FINDING EDEN

A Novella by
By
Pembroke Sinclair

United States of America

First Publication.

Print ISBN 978-1-937809-28-7

Published in the United States of America
Published by
eTreasures Publishing, LLC
4442 Lafayette St.
Marianna, FL 32446
http://www.etreasurespublishing.com

Acknowledgments

To my editors, Cher and Patricia. Thank you for helping me whip this story into shape.

TABLE OF CONTENTS

	Page
DUKE'S JOURNEY	1
LANA'S SALVATION	36
HANK'S INSPIRATION	64
DUKE'S DISCOVERY	90
GOD'S PROMISE	119
Meet the Author	139

DUKE'S JOURNEY

Duke's truck tires squealed as he slammed on the brakes, stopping inches from the garage door. He shut off the engine. The keys fell from his hands to clink to the floor.

"Shoot!"

He smacked his head on the steering wheel, stars danced in front of his eyes, swear words were mumbled under his breath. Holding his forehead, he opened the car door and stepped out. His ankle rolled under him, but he caught himself on the door and chuckled.

"Oooo! Might have had too much to drink." Another laugh escaped his mouth.

With shaky steps, he headed for his house. After two steps, he lurched to the right, almost falling into his hedges. Luckily, the garage was close and held him up. Footsteps sounded behind him. He turned a little too fast, his vision blurring. Someone stood at the back of his truck, a distinctly female outline. Had he brought someone home with him? He typically remembered picking someone up, usually his thoughts focused on how the night would end.

He blinked a few times, clearing his vision. The woman came into view. Duke smiled.

"Heeey, Chanel." He attempted to take a step forward, but swayed back and forth, almost falling on his face. He thought better of approaching her. "What are you doing out this time of night?"

Chanel didn't answer.

Duke's stomach clenched from too much alcohol, the contents threatening to splash out. Chunks slid back down his throat. Water or another drink were a necessity before passing out, but he didn't want to pass up a chance of female companionship. Hopefully, she was just *playing* hard to get.

"You wanna come in and have a drink?"

In response, she gurgled. A low, rumbling sound that originated deep in her throat.

At first, Duke thought maybe she burped, and was taken aback. Chanel was one of those women who didn't leave her house without every hair in place. Was she even capable of producing gas?

His stomach lurched again. His mouth snapped shut, vomit pooled behind his teeth. Covering his mouth with his hand, he choked down bile. He needed to get inside.

"Well, I'm gonna head inside. That offer still stands if you want a drink."

He stumbled toward the stairs. His toe caught on an edge, but he caught himself before falling down. His face reddened, and he glanced over his shoulder. Chanel still stood in the same place, watching his every move. Odd, he thought. What is she doing? But he didn't have long to worry about it. His top priority was getting something to drink.

Duke kept a bottle of orange Gatorade in his fridge for such occasions. Bathed in white fridge light, he downed the entire bottle, liquid running down his chin. He gasped in air when he finished, then let out a long, rumbling burp. Something shuffled in the living room. With a furrowed brow, he glanced into the darkened room. A shadow moved. A smile crossed his lips. He knew she couldn't resist his charms for long.

Pushing the fridge door closed, he stepped into the other room. He contemplated turning on a light, but thought better of it. The hunt would be more fun in darkness. He took another step, the floor rolled under him and he lost his balance. His knee hit first. A dull ache throbbed up his thigh. He was going to feel that in the morning. His shoulder thumped onto the floor, followed by his head. He yowled.

He expected Chanel to rush to his side, maybe turn on a light, to find out if he was all right. Instead, she stood there. What was wrong with her? Didn't she care? Duke rolled onto his hands and knees, crawling to his TV. He punched it on. Flickering light lit the room. He turned to Chanel.

Her arms hung limply at her side, her skin pale. She stared at nothing, her eyes glazed white with dark circles underneath. Her normally flawless hair stuck out in various directions. Mud streaked her Capri pants. Her ripped white shirt exposed a lacy bra. His breath caught.

Instinctively, he crab-walked away from her. He cleared his throat and struggled to his feet.

"Chanel? Is everything all right?"

She turned to face him, but stared right through him. That same throaty gurgle escaped her throat. It almost sounded like a growl. Duke's stomach knotted.

"You know, um, I'm pretty tired. Maybe, ah, we could reschedule that drink for another time."

She stepped toward him. He stepped to his right.

"It was awfully great seeing you, though." He glanced desperately at the front door. Now, how was he going to get her out of it?

She took another step, her mouth falling open. A hiss escaped her lips, determination shrouded her face. Ice formed in Duke's veins. He froze. She lunged forward. She misjudged the distance between them, falling forward. Her nails caught his neck. She dragged them down his flesh. He bolted to the right. Taking steps two at a time, he ran upstairs, and slammed his bedroom door shut. What was wrong with his neighbor? Was she on some type of drug? Footsteps echoed upstairs. Slow, methodical, thudding steps.

He locked the door and glanced around the room. His gaze fell on his gun safe. How would he explain to the cops the amount of alcohol in his system and his dead neighbor? Maybe just pointing a weapon at her would scare her off. But what if it didn't? What if she still came after him? He punched in the combination and took out a rifle and a revolver. Chanel pounded on his bedroom door. Crap. She was relentless. Why couldn't she be that determined to get in his room before getting high? He glanced at the ceiling. It was his only chance. Pulling down the stairs, he scurried into the attic.

Darkness surrounded him. He stared at the floor for a long time, waiting for the door to open. His head grew cloudy, his eyes heavy. Eventually, he drifted into an alcohol-induced sleep while Chanel still pounded on his bedroom door.

***

Duke's eyes opened slowly. His vision focused on the beamed ceiling. Light caught particles of dust, making them sparkle. His skull throbbed. His brain threatened to break it from within. Duke went to lick his lips, but his tongue stuck to his teeth, and his mouth felt like it was stuffed with cotton. He attempted to swallow, succeeding only in making himself cough. He propped himself up on his elbow, trying to catch his breath. Squinting, he took in his surroundings.

A shard of morning sun pierced the small window. What was he doing in the attic? He shook his head, trying to collect his thoughts. A moan sounded from outside. Duke furrowed his brow. That was pretty loud if he heard it all the way up there. He moved to the window.

There were five of them, lurching around on the street. They all had the same glazed-eye look Chanel had, their gray skin sagging on their bones. Was there a party last night? Had they *all* taken some bad drug? He should probably call the police. They could be a danger to themselves and others. Was Chanel still at his door? He placed his ear against the floor, listening. Silence. She must have left. Still, he didn't want to take an unnecessary chance and crawled to the stairs to push them open.

Holding his rifle at his waist, the handgun tucked into his pants, he cracked open his bedroom door. Chanel was gone. He stepped out, glancing downstairs. His front door was wide open. A man from the street crossed in front of it. Duke flattened against the wall. He didn't want to deal with crazed drug addicts. The man outside continued on. Duke hurried downstairs, closing the door softly, hoping he didn't draw any attention to himself.

He hurried to the living room to dial 911. Busy. He hung up and tried again. Same thing. Was it broken? Odd. How could the police station be so busy? Another moan resounded from outside. Duke crouched, trying to make himself smaller, less conspicuous. It wasn't safe in his house. He needed an easily defendable place, maybe somewhere with bars on the windows and a secret way out. But where? He wracked his brain. Ah, the tavern! It was perfect. More than likely, Mitch or Dave would be there. Maybe the phone worked there. If nothing else, they could share a beer and a great story.

Duke hurried to the front door. Cracking it, he peeked out. People were still out there, staggering around, staring at nothing with their milky eyes. Surely, they wouldn't mess with a guy with two guns. They might have been high, but they weren't stupid. Duke took a deep breath before stepping onto the porch.

He stopped at the top of the stairs, squinting from sunlight. His head pulsated. He should've taken some Ibuprofen. No worries, he told himself. The pounding would stop after the first beer. His vision cleared, and he looked at his vehicle. Crap! The door was still open. His truck's interior light had been on all night. The battery was surely dead. His shoulders slumped. Nothing was going his way.

A gurgling sounded to his right. His grip tightened on the rifle's stock. Chanel rounded the hedge, struggling toward him.

"Hey, Chanel. How's it going this morning?"

She groaned in response. Others joined her, creating an unearthly chorus of moans and hisses. They headed toward Duke.

"Now, look, you guys," Duke tried to make himself sound tougher than he felt, but his voice shook slightly. "I don't want to hurt anyone. You all need to back off."

Again, they moaned, continuing forward, making no indication they heard him. They didn't even look at his guns. Duke didn't want to be trapped in his house. There was still enough space between him and Chanel.

He could get to the sidewalk. He stepped downstairs, hurrying past her. They turned and followed after him.

"I mean it. You guys need some serious help."

He fired one shot at the clouds when they continued to advance. The sound should have scared them off. Instead, a barrage of more howls filled the street. Duke turned around to see ten people streaming out of the house across the street. They all had gray skin, glazed over eyes, but several of the new ones had blood-stained clothes. Duke's mouth dropped open. This probably wasn't drug related. He backed away, refusing to take his eyes off the attackers.

He passed a parked car. Something grabbed his ankle. Duke yelled and jerked back, falling into his neighbor's lawn. A man pulled himself out from under the vehicle, grasping at Duke's leg. A chunk of his skull was missing, exposing brain beneath. Duke gasped. Swinging the rifle around, he pointed it at the man. Blood and skull fragments painted the car's door. Duke kicked off the man's body and scrambled to his feet. Close to thirty creatures converged on his position. He had to go. But where? His desire was to go to the bar, but it was too far. A car was his only hope of making it there, especially with those *things* running around. He turned and ran.

A building twinkled before him like a shining beacon. Leaping up the few steps, he grabbed the handle and opened the door. Thankfully, it wasn't locked. A creature lurched out from behind a pillar, swiping its bony hand at Duke's face. Even after slamming the door on the thing's arm, it reached for him. He pushed and strained, but the creature wouldn't relent. Duke grabbed the revolver from his pants. Placing the barrel through the cracked door, he lined up the sights. The man's head snapped backward as the bullet tore through his flesh, his body crumpling. Duke pushed the hand out of the way and closed the door. Just in time. Several more creatures toddled upstairs toward him. After locking the door, he pulled some bookshelves over, just to be safe.

Out of breath but relieved, Duke turned to take in his surroundings. Two stories of bookshelves surrounded him. He was in County Public Library. Not his ideal choice for a hiding place, but it would have to do.

"Hello?"

Only his echo responded.

He walked into an office behind the circulation desk. A water cooler beckoned him. Several cups of water later, he plopped onto a couch. He placed his head into his hands. What was he going to do? More importantly, what was going on? Was this a dream? Did someone lace one of his drinks with a hallucinogen? If he didn't know better, he would say zombies had just attacked him, but that couldn't be possible. Zombies didn't exist.

He ran his hands down his face as he lifted his head. He needed to think about this logically. There was a perfectly good explanation for what was going on. A scientific one. It had to be found. He was in a library, maybe there was a book. He stood and went up to the second floor.

He slowly walked the aisle, unsure what to look for. There were so many books, every title seemed promising. He started with medical books, hoping something would catch his eye. A large encyclopedia would probably be his best bet. There were shelves of them. He picked one and pulled it out. Something fell onto his foot.

"Ouch!"

The edge slammed into his pinky toe. Cursing under his breath, he glanced down. The Bible. Why was that in the medical section? It fell open. He read the passage.

Isaiah 26, verses 19-21: *"But your dead will live; their bodies will rise. You who dwell in the dust, wake up and shout for joy. Your dew is like the dew of the morning; the earth will give birth to her dead. Go, my people, enter your rooms and shut the doors behind you; hide yourselves for a little while until his wrath has passed by. See, the Lord is coming out of his dwelling to punish the people of the earth for their sins. The earth will disclose the blood shed upon her; she will conceal her slain no longer."*

"Oh, my God." He picked it up, rereading the passage. His eyes traveled to the ceiling. "Is this what's happening? Did you do this?"

He hurried out of the aisle and placed the Bible on a table. He examined the other passages around Isaiah 26, hoping one of them would give him a way to combat the threat. Nothing. He slammed the book shut.

"Why?" He yelled upward. "Why are you doing this? What have I ever done to you?"

Silence.

Duke swiped the book onto the floor. Again, it popped open to the same passage. Duke growled.

"You son of a... You answer me! I deserve an explanation!"

A light shimmered above him, forcing him to blink. Were his eyes playing tricks on him? The anomaly was still there. He rubbed his eyes. It remained. His anger dissipated, replaced with fear. What was that? Electricity crackled through the room. Duke's heart rate increased. The light grew in intensity. Duke stepped back, shielding his eyes with his arm. The light flashed, blinding him. He stepped back again, his heel caught on a bookshelf. His arms flew out to his sides, his muscles stiffening, bracing for impact. It never came. Instead, it almost felt like there were hands on his back. He turned, flinching in surprise. His gaze met a woman's.

"There is no need to fear." Her voice was quiet, like the babble of a soft brook.

An ethereal glow surrounded her. Dressed in white robes, her brown hair flowed around her head in ringlets, her wings folded behind her back. Her face looked like porcelain. Her smile was the kindest thing Duke had ever seen. His knees buckled.

"Are you..." The words stuck in his throat. "Are you an angel?"

"God has not totally forsaken you. God is all forgiving. If we repent, He will welcome us back into His grace. Isaiah, chapter fifty-six, verses one to two says, *'This is what the Lord says, 'Maintain justice and do what is right, for my salvation is close at hand and my righteousness will soon be revealed. Blessed is the man who does this, the man who holds it fast, who keeps the Sabbath without desecrating it, and keeps his hand from doing any evil.'''*

"What do you want me to do?"

"You must find Eden. If you find that holy place, you will be saved."

His palms began to sweat, his breath coming in rasps. Was this a hallucination? The desire to pinch himself was overwhelming, but he couldn't move.

"Where? Where do I find Eden?"

"Look for it on the mountain."

The angel's voice faded with her image. Duke remained kneeling. His entire body shook. Did that just happen? Had a heavenly being visited him? He slammed his fist into the bookshelf next to him. Pain radiated up his arm. Nope. It wasn't a dream. It must've been true. Dizzy, he picked up the Bible and used the desk as leverage. Getting to his feet, he headed to the office. He sat down on the couch and began at the beginning.

***

Three days passed as Duke immersed himself in the word of God. He closed the book and stared at the window in the office. He felt renewed, enlightened, and empowered to find Eden. But where to start? There weren't directions or a map, and the angel wasn't too specific about where to look. But the prospect of finding a place where zombies didn't roam free was appealing. They'd stopped pounding on the door days ago, but they were still outside, moaning. It was enough to drive him mad. Maybe it already had.

He stood and headed for the door. Pushing bookshelves aside, he took a deep breath. It was now or never. His hand hesitated on the handle. Should he spend one more day thinking about it? His stomach growled. He didn't have another day. The sparse reserves he found in the building were gone. He needed something more. He wiped the sweat from his brow before jerking open the door.

Sunlight bathed him, and he squinted at the brightness. Ungodly moaning increased as he made his way to the sidewalk. Several creatures were in the vicinity, but he could easily out walk them. Duke headed north, keeping an eye on every building, avoiding parked cars. Two blocks to go, but in that distance, hundreds of zombies could surround him. *Please don't let them get to me.*

He cautiously walked through a car dealership, checking every vehicle, hoping to find keys left in one. A creature milled between vehicles, oblivious to his presence. He looked like a salesman in his khaki pants and tie. Plus, his nametag had the dealership's logo. Duke stayed behind cars, out of the creature's sight. One moan would send others flocking. His best bet was to ensure the undead didn't make a sound. He contemplated shooting it, but that would draw attention too. He needed to stay undetected.

A fluorescent green and silver 1997 Ford F-350 sat apart from the rest, at the end of a row. It drew his attention immediately. He wasn't too optimistic, but he glanced in the window anyway. Keys sat on the seat, twinkling in sunlight. Really? Was he that lucky? He climbed inside. As he closed the door, it stopped on something. He turned. The salesman reached through the door, his mouth snapping open and shut, leaving trails of drool on the window. Duke knew from experience that slamming his hand in the door wouldn't cause him to let go, but he couldn't shoot at that close of range. There was a risk of breaking the window, which he needed for protection. His only other option was to drive off. He turned the key, slamming his foot onto the gas pedal. The truck bounced as the zombie fell under the back tire.

He needed supplies. That was first and foremost on his list. The only place he figured was safe was Wal-Mart on the outskirts of town. With a little luck, zombies had left the area. If not, he'd figure out a way to take care of them. He glanced at the guns sitting on the seat next to him. He had a few bullets left, and he could always get more. Assuming Wal-Mart wasn't overrun with undead.

He sat in the parking lot of Wal-Mart, staring into the store for a long time. Merchandise flowed through broken windows. Sun streamed in from skylights, lighting the store in a gray hue. Duke saw a fair ways into the building, and nothing moved, but that didn't mean a thing. There were hundreds of places a zombie could hide. Yet, he needed to fulfill his mission of gathering supplies. Sighing, he grabbed the shotgun and walked to the door. He hesitated before stepping inside. A short prayer left his lips, asking God to ensure his safety. Holding his breath, he stepped over broken glass.

The smell of rotting food and mold hit him like a brick wall. He covered his nose and mouth to keep from vomiting. Somewhere inside, something metallic clanged onto the tiled floor. He froze. His heart leapt into his throat. Tightening his grip on the stock of his gun, he scanned the area. Nothing moved. No other sounds echoed. He swallowed hard, hoping the lump would leave his throat. It was nothing. Just settling. *There's nothing in here with me.* Steeling his nerves, he grabbed a cart and headed for the grocery section. With time being a luxury Duke didn't have, he went straight to the canned good aisle. Luckily, most of the shelves were still full. Only a few products littered the ground. Without looking at labels, he filled the cart half full with vegetables.

He ran to the next aisle, loading up with soup and canned meat. The cart was almost full, so he went to the chip aisle. He grabbed every bag of jerky in sight, then hesitated for a moment at the nuts. Staring at the cans and bags of almonds, his mouth watered as he thought of their taste. Shrugging his right shoulder, he loaded his arms full of packages. What would a little indulgence hurt? It wasn't a sin if he kept it in reason. Compared to other things he'd indulged in, almonds were the least of his worries.

When his cart was full, he took it out and loaded the truck. He stepped back into the store. A shuffling sounded to his right. He froze and listened. Did he really just hear that? Everything was silent. No, he didn't. His mind played tricks on him. He continued to the camping supplies and gun counter. Duke didn't need to stock up on too many firearms. Guns were nice, but they were only effective if they had ammo. A stash of hundreds of guns was worthless if you didn't have bullets. He grabbed what was needed and threw it all into the cart.

As he moved down an aisle, his eyes drifted over some machetes. He stopped, his eyebrows raised in surprise. Wal-Mart had a lot of stuff, but machetes? Was there a demand for them? He pulled one off the shelf and opened the package. The handle fit nicely in his palm and the weapon wasn't overly heavy. The blade seemed to be sturdy, and the sheath had a strap, allowing him to carry it on his back.

He swung the blade through the air, testing its weight and maneuverability. Something moved to his left. He turned. A zombie stood at the end of the aisle. She looked young, probably no more than nineteen, and she wore her blue Wal-Mart vest. Her left foot dragged behind her, her eyes stared at nothing. Blood matted her blonde hair. It took her a second to notice Duke. She turned. The skin on her cheek had been torn off, exposing the teeth beneath. She raised her hands and came toward him.

Duke rushed forward, swinging the machete. It wasn't exactly how he planned on testing the weapon, but what could he do? One moan would have brought a crowd of zombies. He couldn't afford to be surrounded in the store. The blade sliced three-fourths of the way through her neck before stopping on the spinal cord. She opened her mouth to groan, but her vocal chords had been severed, so an unearthly gasp escaped. A chill ran up his spine. She reached forward and grabbed his shirt.

Duke stared into her lifeless eyes, feeling sorry for her. Underneath the milkiness, she once had bright blue eyes. Before this happened, she was probably a real beauty, the envy of the boys in her class. She clawed at his chest as her mouth snapped open and closed. He pulled the revolver out of his hip holster, placing the barrel a few inches from her forehead. She didn't even notice. She just struggled to get closer. Taking a deep breath, he pulled the trigger. Involuntarily, his eyes squeezed shut, along with his mouth, as ichor sprayed into his face. Her body went limp before falling to the ground, taking the machete with her. Duke's ears rang from the bang. He apologized, said a quick prayer, then headed back to the cart. Three machetes and some sharpeners would suffice. They would be useful in close combat.

After filling his truck with the last of the supplies and cleaning up in the bathroom, Duke climbed back into the driver's seat. Taking back roads, Duke left the city. He parked on a hill, shut off the engine, and observed the destruction. Fires blackened half the buildings, with wisps of smoke drifting skyward. How many lives had been lost? Duke fixed his gaze on the orange, pink, and purple splashes caused by the setting sun.

"You've done some crazy things in your time," he said aloud. "But zombies? Really?" With his hands out to his sides, he chuckled. "I'm not saying the world was perfect. It definitely had its share of sins, but wouldn't a second coming have made more sense?" He placed his hands on the steering wheel and clicked his tongue. "But I'm sure you know what you're doing. I don't know why you saved me, but I'm grateful you did. I'll do my best to make you proud. I'll find Eden."

Duke took a deep breath and leaned back in his seat. He cracked the window, relishing the silence. He pulled out the Bible and let it fall open on his lap.

Isaiah 12:1-3. *"In that day you will say: 'I will praise you, O Lord. Although you were angry with me, your anger has turned away and you have comforted me. Surely God is my salvation; I will trust and not be afraid. The Lord, the Lord, is my strength and my song; he has become my salvation. With joy you will draw water from the wells of salvation.'"*

He settled into his seat and closed his eyes.

A scraping sound pulled him out of a dreamless sleep. He sucked in a sharp breath and jerked, slamming his knee into the steering wheel.

"Shoot!"

He turned the key and prepared to leave. Even though the zombie couldn't get in, the moaning would disrupt his pristine night. He pulled on the lights. A girl was illuminated in the beams. Duke's heart skipped a beat. Instantly, she froze. She shielded her eyes with her right hand and waved with her left. She couldn't have been older than seventeen. Dirt streaked her pale face. Her brown hair was pulled into a ponytail, but half of it hung loose from the tie. Her jacket had a rip on the sleeve, her backpack only had one strap. Duke unlocked the doors.

"Thank you. Thank you so much." She climbed into the cab.

He placed his revolver on his lap. Relief flooded through him to know it was another human, but he wasn't ready to trust her just yet. Her eyes flicked to the gun and back to his face.

"I won't cause you any problems," she said.

The back door opened and slammed. Duke swiveled in his seat, gun barrel raised. No one was going to surprise him. The old man cringed, and Duke almost felt guilty, but how was he supposed to know it wasn't an ambush? He lowered the gun and looked to the female for an explanation.

"This is my friend. He won't cause any problems either." The girl spoke timidly. "We're just looking for a way out of town."

"I apologize. With everything that's going on, I'm a little jumpy." He set the revolver back on his lap. His heart pounded in his ears, adrenaline coursing through his veins. Several deep breaths helped him relax. "You surprised me. What are you doing out this early?"

"We always try to head out before dawn." The girl shrugged out of her backpack. "The cold air makes the zombies move even slower, so we have an advantage.

When we saw the truck sitting here, we thought it was our lucky day. We didn't know someone occupied it."

He smiled. "It is your lucky day. Duke." He held his hand out.

"Lana." She shook his hand. "This is Hank."

Duke glanced over the seat, and the man nodded.

"Where are you two from?"

"A small town about forty miles north," Lana answered. "The only survivors."

"Where are you headed?"

She shrugged. "We don't know, maybe an army base. We figured someone has to be doing something about the undead. What about you? Where are you going?"

"Eden."

She wrinkled her nose. "Well, anywhere has to be better than here. Can we tag along?"

"Of course. Have you eaten yet?"

She shook her head.

"Would you like to?"

Her eyes widened, and she nodded enthusiastically. Duke instructed Hank to slide open the back window and grab some food. Hank complied, handing everyone a can.

"Sorry it's not warm, but it's edible."

Lana opened her top and shoveled in the contents. "I don't mind cold beef stew," she said between bites. "I could eat just about anything right now."

Duke chuckled before spooning cold hash into his mouth.

Half an hour later, they bumped down the road. Hank propped himself on his backpack, snoring away in the backseat. Lana sat with her foot on the dash, staring out the window.

"So where is this Eden?"

Duke shrugged his shoulder. "I'm not exactly sure."

"Well, do you have a map? I can look for it while you drive."

He smiled and glanced at her. "I don't think you'll find it on any map."

She stared at Duke for a moment, her brow furrowed. "You mean Eden isn't a town?"

He shook his head.

She sat in thought for a moment. "You're not talking about Eden like the Garden of Eden are you?"

Duke nodded.

"Isn't it someplace in the Middle East? Like Israel?"

"I don't know. The Bible doesn't give a location."

"Then how are you going to find it?"

"Eden doesn't have to be the exact garden described in the Bible. It is just a place graced by God where all of us sinners can find forgiveness and sanctuary from the undead. I'm looking for that place."

"And just where do you expect to find it?"

"In the book of Isaiah there is a verse, I think it's chapter twenty-five, verses six through eight, that says,

'On this mountain the Lord Almighty will prepare a feast of rich food for all peoples, a banquet of aged wine-the best meats and the finest of wines. On this mountain he will destroy the shroud that enfold all peoples, the sheet that covers all nations; he will swallow up death forever. The Sovereign Lord will wipe away the tears from all faces; he will remove the disgrace of his people from all the earth.' I'm looking for that mountain."

Lana stared at him. He couldn't tell if it was a stare of awe or bewilderment. It would have been nice if it was awe. Another believer would be nice, someone to validate his feelings. He didn't doubt the word of God, but he also didn't want to be the only one who believed it. Silence permeated the cab as he waited for her to speak.

"Are you a priest?"

Duke chuckled. "No."

She adjusted in her seat. Placing her foot on the floor, she faced him. "So, you're looking for a mountain. A mountain God has filled with food and wine and resembles the Garden of Eden?"

"I can tell by your tone you think I'm crazy."

She snorted. "Yeah, a little. I mean, places like that don't exist."

"Maybe it does, maybe it doesn't. But if given a choice to live in a city overrun with zombies where I have to fight for my life every single day or move to mountains where I'm hunting for a mythical city, I'll take my chances in the mountains."

"What gave you the idea to look for Eden in the first place? God doesn't exist. Why would God do this to us?"

Duke contemplated telling her about the angel, but her skepticism told him she probably wouldn't believe him. Half the time, he didn't believe it himself. What if it was a hallucination induced by too much alcohol and stress?

"God exists. You just have to believe. And the Bible has prophesied the end of days for thousands of years. Why is it such a shock when it actually comes about?"

"Revelations talks about the world ending with the Antichrist. I didn't see an Antichrist."

"I'm not talking about Revelations. I'm talking about Isaiah. Old Testament stuff."

He talked about it like a professional because the verses were still fresh in his mind. Only a few days had passed since reading the entire Bible.

Lana shook her head. "Old Testament, New Testament, what does it matter? There is nothing in there that is going to save our souls. We don't even have souls." She turned away, focusing on her nails.

He probably could have said something comforting, but what? If someone told him the same things just days before, he wouldn't have believed them. His new-found faith was just that, new found, and he still had a lot of questions. He couldn't blame her for being skeptical. There were moments he still wondered if he had experienced some kind of psychotic episode. With each moment of doubt, he fell back on his faith, his one constant. Perhaps if he had gone insane, being around others would make it clear. He'd have to wait and see.

By noon, the truck was running low on fuel, and Duke's stomach was growling. It was time to find a place to stop and rest. Buildings were visible on the horizon. A ranch. A great place to pull over. He slowed as he approached the main house and barn. Duke surveyed the area, hoping the rancher would come out to meet him. His stomach knotted when nothing moved. Lana slept but stirred as the truck came to a halt. She leaned forward, looking out the windshield.

"Where are we?" she asked.

"I don't know. Some ranch. I thought a break sounded nice. Plus, we need fuel."

"This isn't a gas station."

"I know. But the truck takes diesel, which is one of the reasons I chose it. Most farms and ranches have their own tanks on property to keep their equipment filled. It keeps us away from population centers where zombies like to congregate."

"Really? I thought maybe you picked the truck for its paint job." She flashed a smile. "Sounds logical. So why are we sitting here? Everything looks quiet."

He sighed. "I know. That's what bothers me. Where are the animals? Where is the rancher? I would have at least expected a dog."

"Maybe he's working in the field," Lana suggested.

"Maybe he's dead," a voice said from the back seat.

"Well, there's only one way to find out." Duke grabbed the rifle from the back and pushed open the door.

A slight breeze stirred the smell of manure and grass. He stared at the house, searching for movement. The windows were dark. Tightening his grip on the gun, he stepped cautiously onto the porch. A board creaked beneath his foot. His palms started to sweat. He went to the door and tried the handle. Locked. Pressing his back against the wall, he side-stepped to the window. With the gun upright against his chest, he peaked through the glass.

Everything seemed to be in its place. Pillows sat nicely on a floral-print couch. Magazines were stacked on a coffee table. Pictures hung neatly on walls, and a vase of flowers adorned the kitchen table at the far end of the room. To his right, a hint of counters peeked from the kitchen, and the sun shone through a back window. A shadow moved across the wall. His breath caught. He pulled his head back, just enough so it was out of view, but not so much that he couldn't still see inside. Minutes passed. Nothing else happened. It must have been a cloud passing by. They were probably safe, but he didn't want to linger too long. If there were zombies around, that would only give them time to find him and his friends. Gravel crunched underfoot as he went back to the truck.

"I think we're all right," he told Lana and Hank. "I'm going to pull around the back side of the barn. I'm guessing the tank is over there."

Duke put the truck in gear and proceeded forward. As they rounded the side of the house, he slammed on the brakes and stared wide-eyed out the windshield. Lana screamed. The rancher and his wife bent over the remains of a cow, their faces stained with blood, the intestines strung between them. The sound of the truck alerted the couple to their presence, and the two converged on their position. The man pounded on the hood, leaving bloody smeared handprints, while the wife limped to the driver's side window.

Lana pulled her knees to her chest and buried her head in her arms. Duke attempted to throw the truck into reverse, to put some distance between them and the creatures, when a shot deafened his left ear. Instinctively, he ducked and covered his head. The rancher moved around the side of the truck. Another shot resounded. The bullet hit the rancher in the shoulder, knocking him back a step, but he didn't go down. He progressed further, and Duke covered his ears, waiting for another shot. A click and Hank swearing under his breath resounded through the howls. When the rancher reached the door, Duke slammed it open with force. The zombie went down with a thud. Jumping out of the truck with weapon drawn, he finished the job. The rancher and his wife lay next to each other in the dirt. He stared at them for a moment before turning to his passengers.

Hank's door was open, and he messed with the cylinder of his revolver. Duke's ear rang, so he couldn't hear what Hank said, but it was something along the lines of "The darn thing keeps jamming!" followed by some other choice words. Lana walked around the front of the truck. She stopped and stared at the bodies.

"Lana, why don't you get back in the cab? You don't need to see this."

Tears streamed down her face. "We can't leave them here," she said quietly. "We have to bury them."

Duke opened his mouth to speak, but Hank interrupted him.

"Now, honey, you know we can't do that. There may be more of them wandering around, and we don't have time." He wrapped his arms around her shoulders and directed her back to the passenger side door. "They'll be just fine where they are." He helped her into the backseat and climbed in after her.

Duke glanced once more at the people–the zombies– on the ground, then climbed in and drove around the backside of the barn. Just as he suspected, a barrel full of diesel sat there. After filling up both tanks, they continued in silence down the road.

About an hour into the drive, Duke couldn't stop yawning and his eyes grew heavy. Lana dozed in the back, and Hank stared out the window. He pulled onto the side of the road. Lana's head popped up.

"What's going on? Where are we?"

"It's all right," Duke told her. "I just need someone to relieve me. Maybe grab a bite to eat."

"I can drive, if you want," Hank offered.

He smiled. "I would like that. Thanks."

Stepping out of the truck, he arched his back. His vertebrae popped and his muscles pulled, almost painfully, and he slowly walked to the bed of the truck. He pulled out some cans of food and a small propane burner. As he dumped the contents into a pan, Hank and Lana joined him.

"Do you really think it's a good idea to stop out here?" Lana asked, wrapping her hands around her chest as she surveyed the area.

"Yeah, we should be just fine. If anything is coming for us, we'll be able to see it miles before it gets here." A smile curled onto his lips, a small gesture to make her feel better.

The chili sputtered in the pan, so he stirred it. Hank stepped closer and sniffed long and hard.

"Smells good."

"Just a few more minutes and it'll be done," Duke told them. He grabbed a sleeping bag out of the back of the truck and unzipped it before setting it in the dirt next to the road, along with some bottles of water and some bags of chips. "Why don't you two have a seat? We'll have a picnic."

Lana hesitated, but Hank readily complied. Duke spooned the chili into bowls.

A cold wind stirred their hair and brought the smell of snow. Soon, it would be fall. Duke closed his eyes and took a deep breath. The promise of salvation and God's word of forgiveness drifted through his mind. He thought about the girl in Wal-Mart and the two at the ranch. They were finally at peace. Hopefully, they went to Heaven, but if they went to Hell, it was what they deserved. Where would Duke go when he died? Based on his actions before the zombie uprising, it would definitely have been Hell. After, though, it was hard to say. Just because he found God didn't necessarily mean he was guaranteed a spot in Heaven. He had to earn it. He would do his best, hoping it worked out for him.

They finished eating and packed their things into the truck. Hank climbed behind the wheel, and Duke sat in the passenger's seat. Lana sat in the back. Hank pulled onto the road, and Duke leaned his head against the headrest, hoping for a little sleep.

"Hey, Duke?"

He felt her breath on his cheek. She leaned forward in her seat, her arms folded on the top of the chair, her chin resting on her hands.

"Yeah?" He didn't open his eyes.

"Why a mountain? Why not a church? Or the beach?"

He took a breath. "Well, I'm guessing it's because it's closer to God. If Heaven is in the clouds, you can't get much closer than the top of a mountain."

"Do you know which mountain?"

He shook his head. "Nope."

"Then how will you know you're there when you get there?"

He faced her. "I'll know. God will give me a sign."

"I sure hope He does." She leaned back in her seat, averting her gaze out the window.

Duke closed his eyes and fell asleep.

They spent the next three days traveling, stopping to get fuel when necessary and having picnics on the side of the road. Luckily, they didn't have another episode. Every night before Duke went to bed, he placed the Bible on his lap and let it fall open. The first night he read Titus 2:5-7, *"he saved us, not because of righteous things we had done, but because of his mercy. He saved us through the washing of rebirth and renewal by the Holy Spirit, whom he poured out on us generously through Jesus Christ our Savior, so that, having been justified by his grace, we might become heirs having the hope of eternal life."*

Night two it was Thessalonians 5:9-10, *"For God did not appoint us to suffer wrath but to receive salvation through our Lord Jesus Christ. He died for us so that, whether we are awake or asleep, we may live together with him."*

And on the third night, Peter 1:8-9, *"Though you have not seen him, you love him; and even though you do not see him now, you believe in him and are filled with an inexpressible and glorious joy, for you are receiving the goal of your faith, the salvation of your souls."*

By this time, they'd climbed in elevation. The air thinned, nights cooled. Zombies were also less abundant. They saw about one once a day–maybe–usually miles away from the side of the road, but they didn't worry about them. Their only concern was road weariness, and they all showed signs. Sleeping in the truck was safe and warm, but they would have given anything to sleep in a bed. And take a shower.

Lana seemed to be the worst. She tried to be patient, but she couldn't. Things only got worse when they hit the Canadian border. Duke stopped the truck at the abandoned border guard huts and surveyed the area. She had been asleep in the back, and she sat up slowly.

"Where are we?" She rubbed her eyes.

"The Canadian border."

Her mouth dropped open. "The Canadian border? Are you kidding me? What are we doing at Canada?"

"I guess this is where we're supposed to go."

She tightened her jaw. "You guess? *You guess?* When are you gonna start knowing? I've been in this stinking truck for three days. How much more do I have to take?" She threw herself down on the seat and stared at the ceiling, her eyes glistened with tears. "It would be really nice if your God would start giving you some answers. At this rate, we'll be driving all over Earth." She rolled away from them.

He looked at Hank, who just shook his head. Lana was right--it would've been nice to know if they were heading in the right direction. Duke had faith that God would lead them to their salvation, but insecurity crept in. Maybe he really had hallucinated the whole thing. But what could he say? He couldn't tell Lana and Hank that. They depended on him. A prayer ran through his mind before he put the truck in gear and crossed the border.

After a few hours, Duke pulled over for lunch. Lana grabbed a bowl of Spaghetti Os and walked 10 feet away, her back to the men as she ate. Goosebumps formed on his flesh as a cool breeze blew, and a thin layer of snow covered the ground. They ate fast, shivering. As they loaded the supplies back in the truck, Duke noticed the rear driver's side wheel was flat. He sighed and pulled out the spare and jack.

"Great!" Lana snarled. "What else could possibly go wrong?" She stomped back to her lunch spot and plopped onto the ground.

Duke gritted his teeth. It was a test, just a test. No one gained salvation easily, it had to be earned. Yes, it was irritating and aggravating, but the end result was worth it. He could–and would–gain redemption.

One of the lug nuts slipped out of his fingers and rolled into the dirt behind him. It stopped on the opposite side of the road. With a sigh, he bent down to pick it up. Something twinkled in the trees below. Out of curiosity, he stepped down the steep incline. Ten steps through the trees, they opened up. Below, a river curled around the base of a mountain, a town lay nestled within the rock walls. Wisps of smoke curled toward the deep blue sky. There were people on the riverbank. The scene was picturesque, surreal. He rubbed his eyes to make sure it wasn't a dream. His heart pounded with excitement. The ground slipped underfoot as he hurried back up the hill.

"Hey! You have to see this."

Lana and Hank followed him back into the trees. Lana clomped the whole way there, her hands folded across her chest. When Hank saw the town, he slapped his thigh and smiled. Lana's hands fell to her side, her mouth open in shock. Oh, good. They saw it too. Duke wasn't imagining it. After a few minutes, she wrapped her arms around Duke's waist.

"You never lost faith." She hugged him tightly. "And look where it got you. You found Eden."

LANA'S SALVATION

Lana stood in front of her locker, staring at her books, deciding which ones she needed for the next few classes. On her right, someone's locker opened with a metallic clink. She smiled at Daphne.

"How's it going today?" Daphne asked.

Lana nodded. "Pretty good. Same as always."

"You going to the dance this weekend?"

Lana moved to close her locker door, when it was ripped out of her hand, slamming shut loudly. She turned, her eyes narrowed at Ben.

"Of course she's not going to the dance this weekend," Ben stated. "Unless it's at the old folk's home."

He turned to Stuart and gave him a high five. They continued down the hall.

"Yeah, should be a great time," Stuart chimed in. "Hey, Lana, do you think they'll play their music on a record player or a phronograph?"

They laughed until they rounded the corner.

"It's phonograph." Lana mumbled under her breath.

"Don't let them get to you," Daphne said quietly. "They're just jerks. They think because they are basketball players and conference champions, they can do anything they want."

Lana flashed her a forced smile before heading to class.

The English teacher droned on about Siddhartha. Lana tried to focus, but her gaze was drawn out the window. Ben trudged across the courtyard. She furrowed her brow. Why was he walking like that? His shoulders slumped forward, his feet dragged, as if he didn't have enough strength to pick them up. His head rested against his right shoulder, his tongue hung out of his mouth. She stared at him for a moment. He just couldn't get enough of messing with people, could he? What kind of joke was he playing? One of these days, someone was going to knock him down a peg. She hoped she was there when it happened.

The classroom door flew open. Daphne entered the room, blood dripping down her neck. What happened? Who hurt her? Lana refrained from jumping out of her seat. She wanted to help her friend, but she didn't want to anger the teacher. Daphne didn't know where she was. She didn't realize there were others in the room with her. Her hands held the door shut, and she cried hysterically. A few students stood from their seats, staring at her. Mr. Lynch approached her. She jumped when he placed his hands on her shoulders and looked at him with unseeing eyes.

"Daphne? What happened? Are you all right?" Mr. Lynch examined her wounds.

Without responding, she collapsed onto the floor.

"Mike, Stan, help me with her." Mr. Lynch turned to the rest of the class. "We're taking her down to the nurse's office. I expect you all to be here when we get back."

The three of them escorted Daphne into the hall. Those left behind burst into quizzical conversation. A few of Lana's classmates walked out. Her stomach knotted and fluttered with butterflies. What was going on? Who attacked Daphne? She looked back out the window. Ben was a few feet from the building. He had dark circles under his eyes, which were glazed white, and a gray pallor to his skin. Her breath caught. She grabbed her bag and left the room. Normally, she followed the rules and listened when teachers or other adults told her to do something. It wasn't in her nature to be defiant. But something extraordinary was going on and she needed to find out what.

She walked to her car. She saw movement out of the corner of her eye. Stuart intercepted Ben. She paused, her hand on the door handle, and watched. Ben lunged at Stuart, his mouth snapping open and closed. Stuart pushed him back, but Ben kept coming after him. She shook her head and opened the door. She'd never understand the relationship between boys. After starting the car, she went to the clinic, leaving the boys to play their silly game.

The parking lot was full. Inside, people cried and bled, demanding medical attention. It looked like the whole town was there. Her mom tried to keep them under control, but it was a losing battle. Lana pushed through the crowd.

"Mom, what's going on?"

"Lana, what are you doing here?" Her mom barely contained her exasperation. "Shouldn't you be at school?"

"Something's going on."

She pursed her lips. "You don't have to tell me."

A patient pushed Lana back. "Wait your turn!" she hissed.

"Lana, wait for me at home. I'll see you there."

A few more patients shoved her away from the desk and toward the door. She stared at her mom for a minute, an overwhelming desire to hug her engulfed Lana's body. How would she get to the counter? If she pushed through the crowd again, she didn't doubt violence would erupt. She wrapped her arms around her chest and stepped through the doors.

Two ambulances pulled up as Lana started her car. She watched them for a moment, her hands sweating as she gripped the steering wheel. This was all too weird. Was there some kind of outbreak? Food poisoning maybe? Her mom told her to go home, but she wanted to make sure everyone at the home was all right first. She put her car in gear and headed for the highway.

The scent of smoke permeated the car. Lana inhaled a deep breath. She liked the smell of campfires. They always made her think of s'mores. The sky turned black as she ascended the last hill before dropping into a valley that contained the nursing home. She slammed on the brakes. Her jaw fell open, her chest tightened.

Orange flames engulfed the main house and storage shed. Small flames licked other buildings. It wouldn't be long until they were inundated. Tears immediately welled up in her eyes. She shook her head. It was a nightmare. It had to be. This wasn't really happening. Lana pushed the accelerator to the floor. She pulled into the dirt driveway and stopped in the parking lot. Why did she think it was a campfire? Who would be camping this time of year? She slammed her hand on the steering wheel twice. What an idiot! She stepped out of her car, noticing another vehicle in the lot. Someone else stared at the carnage.

Lana wanted to ask him what happened but couldn't take her eyes off the fire. She felt nauseous. Her legs were weak, her head spun, and then she collapsed. The other person grabbed her arms, easing her down.

"Just take some deep breaths."

She looked into his face. The wrinkles around his eyes were more pronounced as he furrowed his brow, a slight breeze rustled his gray hair. His hands felt like sandpaper against her flesh, but it was comforting to know someone was there. She tried to obey his request, and sucked in gulps of air. After a few minutes, the black dots disappeared from in front of her eyes. She sobbed.

Lana opened her mouth to speak, but a long, loud moan interrupted her. The pair turned to their right. A nurse stumbled out of the house, her arm and back engulfed in flames. Lana wanted to help. So did the man. They both jumped to their feet. Lana took a few steps before realizing the nurse was beyond help. Shouldn't she be dead? Or in excruciating pain? Her reaction was unnatural. The nurse headed straight for them. The look in her milky eyes told Lana she didn't want assistance. When three more nurses came out of the house, the two of them jumped into Lana's car.

Rocks flew as Lana tore out of the parking lot. Her tires squealed when they contacted pavement. She kept the gas pedal on the floor, barely aware of where she headed. About a mile outside of town, she felt a hand on her arm.

"I don't think we should head back into town."

She eased off the accelerator and pulled onto the shoulder. From their vantage point, they saw people running through the streets, some loading belongings into their vehicles, while others were being attacked and eaten. Her stomach lurched. She barely got her door open before vomit splashed onto the ground.

"I think maybe I'd better drive."

Mechanically, she walked around to the passenger side and climbed into the seat. Leaning her head back, she pulled her knees to her chest and closed her eyes. She wrapped her arms around her midsection. She wanted to protest, to say she had to go to the clinic and get her mom, but something told her it was too late. She wanted to look, too, to see the destruction and carnage, but couldn't force her eyes open. Guilt enveloped her body. She cried again. What was going on? How did things get so bad? The day started out so normal. How did it spin into chaos without warning?

Lana didn't know how long or how far they drove, but they eventually pulled over. She glanced at the surroundings but didn't recognize anything. She sat up and put her feet on the floor.

"Where are we?"

The man sighed. "We're safe. That's all I know."

"What happened?"

He shook his head. "If I didn't know any better, I'd say zombies were attacking."

Lana furrowed her brow. "But that can't be true, right? I mean, there's no such thing as zombies, right?"

He stared at her, eyebrows raised.

They sat for a moment. She stared at her hands, trying to wrap her mind around the fact zombies might have eaten her friends and family.

"You're Lana, right?"

She looked up. "Yeah."

"Hank." He placed his hand flat on his chest. "You probably don't remember me. I'm Gladys's husband."

Realization came slowly. "Hank. I remember you. Came every Tuesday and Saturday at three."

He nodded. "Yep, that's me."

He turned his gaze out the windshield. Lana studied him for a second. Black soot smeared his face, ash covered his shirt. His eyes were red and irritated. Was he in the home when it caught fire? Lana didn't ask out loud. For all she knew, he could've started the blaze. Of course, she didn't really believe that. His hands shook and grief shrouded his face. He acted like a man who had just lost everything, not like a lunatic who purposely took something away.

"What are we going to do?" she whispered.

Hank took a deep breath. "I don't know. Maybe we can find someone. Figure out what's going on. There's an army base not far from here. Maybe they can help."

She nodded slowly. "Maybe. How far away is it?"

"Couple hours. Once we get there, they'll be able to explain what's going on, and everything will be just fine. You'll see."

He put the car in gear and continued down the road.

***

As they approached the base's gate, hope drained from Lana's body. No one stood in the guard hut. The barricade arm was upright. There weren't any vehicles in the yard. Hank slowed and glanced into the hut before proceeding toward the barracks.

"Maybe they were called out to the main base. It's possible they are pooling their resources before sending out cleanup crews."

Lana doubted that highly. Why wouldn't they take care of the problem right now? Why did they have to pool resources? They were going to die. The zombie horde was going to eat them. She wanted to sit and wait.

"We should head in. Maybe someone was left behind to let others know what's going on."

Lana sighed. "You go. I'll wait here."

"Okay. I'll be right back." He opened the door and disappeared into a building.

Leaning her head against the window, she pulled her knees to her chest. Hank was gone for a while, she wasn't sure how long. She didn't turn when the door opened and Hank climbed in.

"Looks like they left in a hurry. Everything is still in their foot lockers."

"Maybe they're all dead."

Hank sighed. "They're not dead. I didn't see any bodies."

Keys jingled as he turned the ignition. A click sounded, not the expected roar of an engine. Lana looked over her shoulder as fear rose in her chest. Hank turned the key again. Nothing. Not even a click. She sat up.

"I don't know what's wrong," Hank said, reading her mind. "But it'll be dark soon. We should probably settle into one of these barracks."

She glanced from him to the empty building in front of them. Her stomach knotted, her skin prickled. The last thing she wanted was to go into an abandoned building. They didn't know what happened to the soldiers. What if zombies hid in there, waiting for more victims? But she also knew they didn't have any other choice. She wanted even less to walk down an unlit highway at night. At least in the building, they'd see an attack coming.

She felt weird being in barracks with all of the soldiers' stuff. What would happen if they came back? Would they be angry at them for trespassing? When the sun went down, shadows chilled the room. She wrapped her arms around her chest as she sat on a bed.

"Here," Hank said. "I found this coat in a locker. It'll keep you warm."

She pushed her arms into the sleeves of the puffy down coat, feeling even more bizarre for wearing someone's clothes. She checked the pockets. Nothing. Good, maybe no one will miss it if she took it. Hank found some crackers, but everything else was gone. They ate silently. The crackers were slightly stale and did little to satiate her hunger. At least she wasn't alone. She wouldn't have made it by herself.

"You should get some sleep."

She swallowed thickly. "I don't want to."

He patted her knee. "You'll be fine. I won't let anything happen to you."

He sat in front of the door with an emergency ax he found in one of the other bunkhouses on his lap.

Lana placed her head on the pillow. Every time she closed her eyes, she saw the nursing home in flames or her classmates with blood running down their faces. She worried about her mom. What happened to her? Did she get out of the clinic? Or did the creatures devour her behind the admissions desk? Her heart rate increased, tears threatened to fall. She wasn't going to sleep.

The pink hue of morning peeked through the windows. Hank stood from the chair and arched his back. Lana sat up on the bed. Without saying a word, they stepped outside the barracks. The air chilled her bones. She was glad to have a coat. Hank found one too. They tried to start the car one more time. When that didn't work, they started their walk on the highway.

They followed it until midmorning. The air warmed quickly, causing Lana to sweat. She draped the coat over her arm. It was bulky and cumbersome, but she knew she would need it later. Otherwise, she would have left it. Lana was tired, hungry, and her feet hurt. How much longer did she have to endure this torture? She wanted to stop and rest, but Hank said they had to keep moving. Eventually, they came to a gas station. Her stomach growled audibly, and she felt renewed energy surge through her body. She took two running steps, barely able to contain her need for food, before Hank grabbed her arm.

"Not so fast, Lana. We have to make sure there aren't any creatures in there." He scurried to a bush on the side of the road and crouched behind it.

Lana wanted to scream or cry because she was so hungry she couldn't stand it. She was sure her stomach would fall out of her body if she didn't eat soon. She tried to overcome the frustration and followed him, plopping down into the dirt. They sat there for an eternity before he finally said it looked safe. She barely had enough strength to get to her feet, but somehow she made it to the store. Ecstasy overtook her when she stepped through the front door. She found a cooler with water and downed a whole bottle before grabbing another. She opened it on the way to the jerky aisle. Grabbing a bag, she tore it open with her teeth. She couldn't shovel meat in fast enough. Hank was on the other side of the store.

"What are you doing?" Lana asked with a mouth full.

"Loading a backpack with supplies."

"Good idea."

She filled a pack with jerky, chips, and water. She stopped for a moment in front of the pop cooler. What would it hurt if she grabbed a couple Sunkists and some

Red Bull? They might come in handy if they had another sleepless night.

When she finished, she met Hank at the front of the store. The straps of her bag dug into her shoulder. If she put even just one pack of gum in it, she would've tipped over. Looking over at Hank, he seemed to be in the same situation. His shoulders slumped as he strained under the weight. Should they find another vehicle? It would carry all their supplies so they didn't have to. How would they get one? Lana didn't know how to hotwire a car, and, more than likely, Hank didn't either. Besides, they probably shouldn't take someone else's property. The owners might need it just as bad as they did.

"You ready?" Hank asked.

Lana stared into the empty parking lot at the gas pumps for a moment and sighed. Where were they going to go? Did he really think the military could help? Shouldn't they already be doing something? She doubted there was any place safe, doubted they had any chance of survival on their feet. But what other choice did they have? If they stayed any place for too long, they risked zombies finding them. There was also the chance there were other survivors. The only way to find them was to look for them. She turned and nodded.

They traveled all day, sticking close to the highway but not actually walking on it. Hank explained it would be safer in the brush in the ditch. By noon, Lana's shoulders were on fire and her feet dragged. Why had she packed so much food? Did she really think she'd need it all? Black clouds covered the sky, small sprinkles of rain moistened her face. She stopped and pulled on the coat. The padding helped relieve some of the pain, and it protected against the wetness. A few minutes later, rain came in torrents. The coat became heavy and smelled like a wet dog. She desperately wanted to find shelter, but Hank said they had to keep moving.

After two hours, she had enough. She knew they were close to a town or city because a bunch of abandoned vehicles littered the road. Soaked to the bone and cold, she thought climbing into a car sounded like a good idea. She didn't wait for Hank's approval. Hightailing it to the closest vehicle, she grabbed the handle.

Hank yelled at her, but she couldn't hear him over the downpour. Lana opened the door, then turned back to him. A creature grabbed her wrist. She screamed, shutting the door on its arm before it had a chance to get out. It had a death grip on her sleeve. Hank hurried to her side and helped push.

The zombie would not let go of her coat, no matter how hard they pushed against the door. Obviously, it couldn't feel pain. It struggled against the car. A loud, low moan that sent shivers down her spine escaped the undead's mouth. Hank pulled out the ax and chopped at the forearm. Lana pulled back, afraid to get cut, and ripped the coat and strap of her bag. She fell. The car door swung open. The zombie slithered onto the ground and crawled toward them. Hank grabbed Lana's arm, pulling her to her feet. Another moan sounded. She glanced at the highway. More zombies lurched toward them. Her heart jumped into her throat. Her brain screamed for her to run, but she couldn't move her legs.

"We have to move, now!" Hank tugged at her sleeve. It was just enough momentum to get her moving. They ran to a grove of trees next to the road.

They found a large oak with sturdy branches and scrambled up. Hank lost his backpack. It was too heavy for him to climb with, so he slipped out of it. Zombies assembled at the base. They clawed and pounded on the trunk, but they couldn't climb up. Lana and Hank sighed with relief. A few of them thought Hank's bag was a quick meal, and tore it to shreds, spilling the contents onto the ground. Better the backpack than one of them. Lana leaned her head back and took several deep breaths. She learned her lesson. No matter how tired and wet she was, getting into a strange car was a bad idea.

Around four in the afternoon, the rain stopped and the sun came out. Creatures still milled around, moaning loudly, but they couldn't get Lana or Hank. The tree's branches were wide, so they took off their coats and settled in. They weren't going anywhere anytime soon, so they got as comfortable as possible. Lana placed her coat in the sun and lay next to it. The rays warmed her chilled skin. If it weren't for the zombies, she could've taken a nap.

She watched the creatures and thought about luck. Really, she and Hank were lucky to get away from them. She counted 15. They were slow, but there were a lot of them. How long would they stay down there? Hopefully, they would grow weary of the pursuit and move to find easier prey. Then, they could get away.

Night fell, and the creatures still roamed below them. Lana shivered as the air cooled. She pulled her coat back on. The afternoon sun dried it a little, but it was still pretty wet and slightly uncomfortable. The scent of wet dog lingered. She had to make do, though, since she had nothing else. She growled under her breath, folding her arms over her chest.

"Do you think they'll ever leave us alone?"

"I don't know, Lana. I just don't know."

Sheer exhaustion took over, and she eventually fell asleep.

She awoke just before dawn. Her butt had fallen asleep, and her bladder threatened to explode. She sat up and looked over the edge. Zombies were still below them. Thankfully, they had stopped pounding on the tree and groaning. They had moved away from the trunk, just enough so Hank and Lana could sneak by them. They were also having trouble moving. A thin frost covered them and the ground.

"Hank," she whispered. "You up?"

"Yeah."

"I think we can outrun them."

He sat silently for a moment. "I don't know if that's a good idea. Where are we going to go?"

"I don't know, but we can't stay here forever. Maybe we can head deeper into the trees. Maybe there are some cabins we can get to."

Again, there was a pause. "All right. I will follow you."

She pulled the bag onto her back and slid cautiously down the tree. Zombies tried to come after her, but they couldn't. Their knees were stiff, refusing to bend. One fell over, causing others to topple over it. Hank and Lana got away from them with a brisk walk. Lana smiled with satisfaction as she glanced over her shoulder.

***

They traveled for two days, starting their excursions before dawn. At night, they slept in trees. On the third morning, Lana spotted a truck sitting on a hill. It was their lucky day. Finally, she convinced Hank it would be faster to travel by vehicle. They hadn't seen another living soul, so she was pretty sure no one would miss their property. They just had to find a car with keys left inside, preferably one that wasn't in a city and surrounded by hundreds of undead. A vehicle was also safer. They wouldn't have to continue sleeping in trees. Lana's butt would surely thank her. Aside from safety issues, they were also running low on food. Her hunger was almost unbearable, and Lana didn't think she could make it another step. In a car, she wouldn't have to expend her precious energy.

They approached with caution. After the last encounter, she wasn't going to run up to any unknown vehicle. They crouched in bushes and watched for a while. She didn't see any movement on the inside. Still crouched, she waddled to the passenger door. Rising cautiously, she peeked in. Dark. She tried the handle. Locked. She decided to try another door. As she walked around the front of the truck, the lights flashed on. She consciously willed herself not to pee her pants. Frozen in the light, she knew exactly what a deer felt like. Someone moved in the cab. It had to be a live person. Zombies didn't know how to turn on lights.

The first day Hank and Lana traveled with Duke, they stopped at a ranch for fuel. She'd never forget that day. It had been ingrained in her mind. Not just because they ran into zombies who were feasting on a cow, but because of what happened later in the night. Lana had a hard time sleeping. Every time she closed her eyes, she saw blood and guts and the rancher and his wife with their milky eyes. She couldn't get the image of their outstretched arms and snapping jaws out of her mind. Something clicked in the cab. Duke sat with a book light and his Bible. She watched silently as he set it on his lap, letting it fall open.

"You really think you're going to find answers in there?"

He looked at her and smiled. "I don't know. But I find it comforting."

She sat up and glanced at the page. "What does it say?"

"It's James one, verses two through four. *'Consider it pure joy, my brothers, whenever you face trials of many kinds, because you know that the testing of your faith develops perseverance. Perseverance must finish its work so that you may be mature and complete, not lacking anything.'*"

She stared at him for a moment. "So this is a test?"

"Seems to be. I guess God was fed up with humanity's lack of faith, so He developed a means to bring us back into the fold."

She scoffed. "Seems like a lot of trouble to go through for a few followers."

He closed the Bible and faced her. "What happened to you? How did you lose your faith?"

She sat silently for a moment, looking at him. The glow from the book light cast an orange hue onto his features. The smile vanished from his lips. Sadness covered his face. Normally, Lana didn't like to talk about her lack of faith. She found out a long time ago it raised disdain and made her appear weirder than she already was. She sighed.

"When I was three, my mom got a job at a nursing home outside of my hometown. It was called Peaceful Souls. Since she couldn't afford daycare, she took me with her. The elderly people loved to ooh and aah over me. I loved the attention."

She placed her chin on her hands, smiling at the memory. Peaceful Souls was her second home. She was close with the residents, often telling them stories and asking for advice. They were her friends, her confidants. She never knew anyone more friendly or loyal.

After she started school, the bus dropped her off in front of the nursing home. She stayed with her mom until the end of her shift, then they'd both go home. They did this for several years until her mom transferred to the new clinic in town. That happened during Lana's freshman year of high school, but she continued to visit the home. She still took the bus out there, and her mom picked her up later. Sometimes, the weather would be so bad she had to stay, but she didn't mind. They always had a bed ready for her in the nurses' quarters. When Lana finally got her own car, her mom never had to worry about picking her up.

Lana never really had a lot of friends, mainly because other kids thought she was weird for staying at the nursing home. Like so many people in society, they didn't understand. When the old folks lived out their usefulness, they were sent away. Since Peaceful Souls was so far away from normal town life, most people put the place out of their mind. There weren't a lot of visitors. Her mom always used to say, "Out of sight, out of mind. That's how families get through their day."

Lana never really understood that phrase until she was older. Then, it made her sad. Most of the people at the home were the coolest she'd ever met. They shared such wonderful stories, and they'd experienced so much. How could anyone just abandon them? She looked forward to every day with them.

It wasn't always sunshine and wonderful memories, though. Death happened. What else would you expect from an old folks' home? Lana remembered the first death she dealt with. She was in kindergarten, and her name was Mrs. Hersh. The day before it happened, Mrs. Hersh showed Lana pictures of herself as a little girl and told her a story about bunnies. She climbed through a bush and saw the mother rabbit and babies in a clearing. Her mother was there, too. She was in the middle of telling the story for a second time when Lana's mother came in and told Lana it was time to go. Lana whined and cried. She wasn't ready. She wanted to hear the story again. Mrs. Hersh promised to retell it the next day. Lana barely sat still in school that day. She ran out the bus door before it opened all the way and into the building. Dropping her backpack and coat off with her mom, she hurried to Mrs. Hersh's room. Normally, she got there just as Mrs. Hersh woke from a nap, so she opened the door slowly and peered in.

An orange hue lit the room as the sun peeked through her closed shades. Silence pervaded, the faint smell of urine lingered in the air. Something was wrong, but Lana didn't know what. Her hand fell from the handle, she stared at Mrs. Hersh's back for several long moments. Finally, she took a deep breath and stepped inside. Lana walked around the bed. Mrs. Hersh's eyes were closed, her face gray. Delicately, Lana touched Mrs. Hersh's cheek. It was still warm, but the heat quickly drained from her skin.

"Mrs. Hersh." Lana shook her shoulder. "Wake up."

Lana knew she wasn't going to open her eyes. She couldn't stop tears from flowing. She kissed the old woman gently on her forehead, then headed down to her mom, making sure she closed the door softly behind her.

That death wasn't the last. Lana experienced several of her friends leaving. It was sad, but it was also a relief. After the first few deaths, her mom took her to church. She thought it would help Lana understand what happened. At first, she really enjoyed hearing stories about Heaven and how they were going to a place without pain, but after a while, she thought God was cruel. If He existed, why would He let people in Peaceful Souls suffer alone? Why would He let their families abandon them? Lana watched them anguish, saw how their hearts broke, and she couldn't believe God would allow that to happen.

"I quit believing," she shrugged.

"I can't believe you turned from God because you thought He gave up on those people." Duke's voice was soft, barely over a whisper. "He never gave up. He gave them you. You became their families, their hope, their light. You gave each and every one of them peace before they went to Heaven. You were their angel."

She opened her mouth to speak, but snapped it shut. Was this guy crazy? She wasn't a servant of God. God abandoned her and everyone else a long time ago.

"Then why did God let them all die in a fire?"

"He spared them. Would you have wanted them to have to witness this? Or fall prey to the living dead?"

"Then why didn't God save us? Why are we here to witness this?"

"He will. We just have to trust in His plan." He turned back to his Bible and let it fall open. "Jeremiah, chapter twenty-nine, verses eleven. *'For I know the plans I have for you,' declares the Lord, 'plans to prosper you and not to harm you, plans to give you hope and a future.'*"

"Well, you believe whatever you have to in order to get through this, and I'll believe what I have to." She rolled away from him, pretending like she was going to sleep.

Duke closed the book and clicked off the light.

Lana still couldn't sleep. She wanted to believe what Duke told her. She wanted to believe there was hope, but too many bad things had happened. She wasn't an angel. She went to the nursing home because she felt sorry for those people. Plus, she never had any friends. She didn't know how to relate to kids her own age. Besides, she didn't know anything else. It was her mom's fault. If she had only let her go to daycare like a normal kid, she would've had friends. *Whatever!* she thought. *There's no sense dwelling on it.* She couldn't change anything. She pushed the thoughts from her mind and fell into restless dreams.

Sun pierced through the truck window, hitting Lana right in the face. She groaned and rolled toward the seat, attempting to hide her eyes under her arm. Laughter and muffled voices resounded outside, followed by dishes clinking. Duke and Hank were already awake, fixing breakfast. She sighed with disdain. She opened the car door and stepped out. The air was cool, and the breeze caused goosebumps to form on her flesh. She wrapped her arms around her chest and jogged a few steps in place. The guys turned and looked at her.

"Good morning, star shine," Hank said.

Lana smiled, hiding her grumpy attitude. It wasn't Hank's fault she didn't sleep. She shouldn't take her anger out on him. She could grin and bear it until they got on the road. After that, everyone would lose themselves in their own thoughts, and she could focus on her anger in peace.

They ate breakfast in silence. While Duke put the food and cooking supplies away in the back of the truck,

Hank intercepted her as she climbed into the truck. His hands were in his pockets as he dug a small hole in the dirt with the toe of his shoe.

"He's right, you know?"

"Who's right?"

"Duke. You were those peoples' angel. Gladys told me all the time how much she enjoyed your visits. She told me how you made her laugh. She was always happier after she talked to you." He averted his gaze downward. "I never wanted to put her in the home, but I didn't have a choice. I couldn't take care of her anymore. I was too weak. She told me she understood and she wasn't mad, but a light in her eyes dimmed when I left her at Peaceful Souls. Due to my illness, I couldn't visit as much as I wanted to either." He placed a hand on her arm. "But I could always tell when you had visited. She smiled more and the light returned. You did. You saved those people."

Lana didn't know why, but after hearing those words, she became really embarrassed and then really angry. She pulled out of his grasp and climbed into the truck. Throwing herself onto the seat, she turned away from them. So what if she was their angel? That didn't save her. She was still stuck in hell with the walking dead. God may have saved all those people, but He left her to rot. At that moment, she stopped doubting His existence. She needed Him to be real because she needed to be mad at Him.

The front doors closed, and the truck moved. Something thumped on the floor. She rolled over. Duke's Bible fell open to Psalm 22, verses 1-2. *"My God, my God, why have you forsaken me? Why are you so far from saving me, so far from the words of my groaning? O my God, I cry out by day, but you do not answer, by night, and am not silent."* She slammed the book shut and rolled back over.

Over the next few days, Lana stewed in her anger. When they reached the Canadian border, she couldn't take it anymore. Why was God doing this? Why was He making it so hard to be saved? How much more suffering did they have to endure? The flat tire put her over the edge. She walked away from Duke and Hank so she could curse God. As she sat there, grinding her teeth, a rabbit poked its head out of its hole. Its nose wiggled in the wind for a moment before it hopped to some grass and nibbled away. Lana thought of the story Mrs. Hersh told her.

As a girl, probably no more than seven, her family took her to town to participate in an Easter egg hunt. She saw an egg under a bush and went to grab it. She bent down and saw a mother rabbit with her babies. She stopped to watch them for a while. Mrs. Hersh must have been gone longer than she thought because she heard her mother's voice frantically calling for her.

"I stepped out of the bushes and waved at my mother," Lana remembered her saying. "Then I signaled for her to follow me into the bushes."

Mrs. Hersh and her mother sat there watching the rabbits for a long time.

"She held me on her lap," Mrs. Hersh recalled, "her mouth right next to my ear, and she whispered, 'Jesus died so we could be saved from sin. Easter is a time of resurrection. These baby bunnies remind us that God will always give us new life.'"

Lana almost burst into tears as she thought about the story. Luckily, Duke called for them to follow him into the trees, so she pulled herself together.

She was speechless when she saw the village. Suddenly, everything made sense, and her anger melted away. She climbed into the truck, accidentally kicking open the Bible. She glanced at the passage. Psalms 71:20-21. *"Though you have made me see troubles, many and bitter, you will restore my life again; from the depths of the earth you will again bring me up. You will increase my honor and comfort me once again."*

She smiled and glanced out the window. Things were going to be all right. They *were* going to be saved.

They followed the road to Eden. Lana stared at Duke through the rearview mirror. He wasn't always a righteous man, she knew that. If he had been, he wouldn't still be there. What changed his mind? Was there a rabbit in a field somewhere that made him see the light? He could probably teach her a lot. If he was willing to instruct, she would learn. Their gaze met through the mirror and Duke smiled.

HANK'S INSPIRATION

Hank sat in the small room on the examination table, paper crinkling beneath him. He hated starting his day at the doctor's office. There were so many other things he could be doing. Besides, he always ended up waiting twenty minutes for the doctor to talk to him for five. It was such a waste of his time, and he didn't have a lot of it left. It's not like they told him anything new. At 73, the only thing that would be news was that he was going to die, but the news probably wouldn't overly shock him. He sighed and hunched his shoulder forward. How much longer?

Shouting sounded in the hall. With the door shut, the voices were muffled. Someone else must have been upset about the doctor's schedule. Hank huffed. That outburst would probably set him back another twenty minutes. Dr. Toth burst through the door, Hank's chart in his hand. Hank's eyes widened.

"Hank, it's good to see you. Do you mind if we reschedule? We seem to be having a bit of an emergency out there. Is that all right with you?"

Hank shrugged and nodded. "Yeah. I can handle that." If it got him out of there faster, he was happy.

Dr. Toth forced a smile. "Great. If you see the receptionist, she'll get you all set up." He left the room as quickly as he entered.

Hank went to the lobby, but the receptionist was busy. At least 10 adults crowded her window, demanding to see a doctor. Several others sat in the waiting room, their eyes wide, their skin pale. One particular individual bled profusely from a wound on his chest. His head hung on the back of his chair, his mouth gaping. Hank was sure he was dead. Nurses came out with a stretcher and grabbed him. A moan escaped the man's lips, his head rolled to one side, so Hank knew he was alive. Mothers hugged gray frightened children. What was going on? He could've waited for the receptionist, but other patients started yelling and cussing, so he left. He would call for an appointment later. Maybe.

He got home and decided to do a little yard work. The day was sunny and warming up nicely, but it wasn't too hot yet, so he needed to weed the flowerbeds. Gladys hated it when weeds choked her lilies. He grabbed the trowel and gloves out of the garage, then searched for his knee pad. It was supposed to be on the hook. Where did it go? He looked behind a shelf and on the floor. As he searched, a scream resounded next door. He ignored it. Whatever happened was none of his business. Then, the neighbor, Macy, ran into his garage.

Why did it have to be her? She was a disrespectful teenager who dressed like a tramp. Her boyfriend always brought her home late, his stereo thumping with noise. Hank told him on at least two occasions to turn his crap down, but he was pretty sure the punk didn't hear him. She always fought with her parents too. But, it was none of his business, so he stayed out of it. He grumbled under his breath, continuing to look for his knee pad. Maybe she'd take the hint and go away.

She stood there, in her too small black shorts with pink skulls and a black tank top. Her black hair, with its pink and purple ends, stuck up in all directions. She trembled, her face pale. Why wasn't she in school? Why was she standing in his garage in her pajamas? He glanced at his watch. 8:30. School had started twenty minutes ago.

"Please, help me," she spoke quietly.

Blood dripped down the back of her arm. He wanted to send her home, but she looked so desperate. With a sigh, he signaled for her to go into the house. He was probably going to regret it. She practically ran through the door, then slammed and locked it behind him. She went to the living room and looked out the window before closing the curtains.

"All right, all right, Macy. Have a seat on the couch. I'll get something to clean up your arm."

Hank walked into the bathroom and grabbed a washcloth, along with some rubbing alcohol. He wet the cloth down before heading back. Macy sat on the edge of the couch, her hands tucked between her knees, flinching at every sound. Sitting next to her, Hank wiped at the blood. Someone had bit her. It looked pretty bad.

A huge chunk of her flesh was missing; black streaks snaked through her veins. He poured some alcohol onto the cloth and pressed it against her skin. She jerked her arm.

"Aren't you even going to ask what happened?" She stared at him wide eyed.

"Should I? I figured it's none of my business."

Macy jumped up. "My father attacked us! We were sitting at the kitchen table eating breakfast, and he bit my arm. My mom tried to get him off, and he went for her neck. I have no idea what's gotten into him." She collapsed back onto the couch. Tears moistened her eyes. "Do you think my mom's all right?"

"I don't know. Let me get you a dressing, then I'll go over and find out." He stood and went back to the bathroom.

While Hank searched the cupboards for some gauze, he heard Macy talking. He poked his head out. She was on the phone. With any luck, she called the police, but that would have been too much to ask for. He was sure the dye she put in her hair short circuited her brain. She sat on the couch when he returned with the gauze.

"I really appreciate this, Hank."

He cringed, keeping his focus on the bandage as he wrapped her arm. "It's no big deal. You might want to go to the clinic to get that checked out. It looks like it might be infected."

She nodded. "I will."

Hank heard her boyfriend's car before it even pulled up in front of his house. He stared at her, his head cocked to one side. Was she really that dense? Her dad went insane and attacked them, and the person she calls is her lazy, no-good, deadbeat boyfriend?

"Don't you think you should talk to the police? Maybe wait here until I find out what's happened to your parents?"

The car stopped right outside his window, the bass threatening to shatter the glass. The punk honked the horn, one long loud beep.

She shook her head. "If they're all right, they'll know where to find me. Tell them to call." She jumped from the couch and headed to the front door.

He watched from the window as the black car peeled down the street, cursing under his breath. What if they're not all right? What then? When they were out of sight, Hank went to the kitchen and picked up the phone, dialing 911. A busy signal. With eyebrows furrowed, he tried again. Same thing. He hung up and went to his bedroom. Grabbing the .44 magnum from the box under his bed, he checked the cylinder for bullets. All six chambers were full. He headed across his lawn to the neighbors' house.

Macy left the front door open, so he approached carefully. He walked through the living room to the dining room on the right. Cereal bowls sat on the table, along with a coffee cup. They had all spilled, and the liquid swirled onto the floor. The tang of iron hit his nostrils. As he rounded the table, he found Macy's mom. Her throat had been torn out, and blood pooled around her. Scuffling resounded from the kitchen. He raised his gun and approached. He stopped and placed his back against a wall, peeking around the corner. Macy's dad paced back and forth between the sink and the island, blood dripping down his chin. Yellow tinted his skin, and his eyes were glazed white. Hank turned away, taking a deep breath.

What was going on? Had the stress of his job finally hit him? Was he high on drugs? If Macy's dad was insane or hopped up on dope, there was no way Hank could take him. Best to leave things to professionals. Macy's dad hadn't seen him, and nothing could be done for the mother, so Hank left the house and headed for his car. He could've shot the man, made him pay for what he did to his wife, but he had vowed never to kill another human being. Besides, it wasn't his place to judge. He needed to get away. With a crazy man next door, it wouldn't take much for him to turn his rage on his neighbors. Gladys would know what to do. He could call the police from the home.

***

Chaos ruled the nursing home. Doctors rushed around gathering medical supplies, nurses attempted to keep patients calm. No one stopped him as he entered. Normally, guests had to sign in so the nurses could keep track of who the patients were with and where they were. They didn't want anyone inadvertently escaping. Or being kidnapped. He went straight to his wife's room. She sat in her chair, her afghan on her shoulders, staring out the window. She smiled as he approached.

"Hank, darling, what are you doing here?"

He smiled back, trying to keep the worry off his face so she didn't become concerned. "I had some time, so I thought I would come and see how you were doing."

"But it's not Saturday."

He knelt next to her. "I know, sweetie. I know. How would you feel about going for a drive?" The country was just the place to clear his head and ask Gladys's advice about the neighbors.

She straightened up in her seat. "Oh, that sounds lovely. Do you think we can go through the canyon?"

He nodded. "Of course. Anywhere you want to go."

Shouts echoed outside her door. Gladys shook her head.

"It's been like this for ten minutes now. I guess there's some emergency back in town. All of the doctors have been called into the clinic. Have you heard anything?"

He shook his head. What could he tell her?

"Well, no matter. One less person for them to worry about will be all the better. Just let me tell Cynthia I'm going for a drive." Gladys pushed the knob on her chair and headed for the door. Hank grabbed the handles on the back and stopped her.

"Gladys, I think it'll be all right if you just leave. They're pretty busy right now."

She smiled again. "Oh, you're probably right. Besides, we'll be back by lunch."

"Sure. Whatever you want. I just have one thing to do first." He picked up the phone, dialing 911. Again, there was a busy signal. Frowning, he hung up and took his place behind his wife's chair.

"What was that about?" she asked.

"I'll tell you in the car."

He opened the door. Black smoke engulfed them. Orange flames covered the walls at the end of the hall. Gladys grabbed his hand.

"Hank! What's going on?"

"Something's caught fire."

"You have to do something. Call someone. Why aren't they evacuating the building?"

He pushed Gladys toward the nurses' station, but didn't make it far. Thick smoke sent them both into coughing fits. He took her back to her room and tried the phone again, just to make Gladys feel better, but he knew what would happen. No signal. Flames flickered under the door, the heat intensified. He paced the room, trying to figure out his next move. Where was everyone? Why weren't they trying to evacuate the residents? He glanced out the window and at Gladys. Could he possibly lift her out the window? Would he be able to carry her to the car? She must have known what he was thinking. She grabbed his arm.

"Go, Hank. Save yourself. There's nothing you can do for me."

He knelt in front of her. "I won't leave you here alone. Not again."

She placed her hand on his cheek. "You did what you had to do. I'm not angry with you and I don't hate you." She kissed his lips. "I love you." She pulled off her wedding ring and handed it to him. "You have to make sure Lana gets this."

Hank kissed her again, and then held her for a long time. Why was Lana supposed to get her ring? It was best not to question Gladys's requests. He rose and headed to the window. He slid it open, then turned back to his wife. Despite Gladys's protests, he couldn't leave her there. Placing his hands under legs, he lifted her from the chair. She squirmed in his arms.

"What are you doing?"

"I'm not leaving you here. Not like this."

The roof creaked. There wasn't much time. He turned to the window. The dang thing slid shut. He placed Gladys back in her chair.

"One minute. I have to open the window."

He pushed open the glass, and just as he turned back, the ceiling collapsed, burying her in rubble.

"No," he breathed. "No!"

He ran forward, but more of the roof collapsed and flames licked his arms. With tears in his eyes and a heavy heart, he climbed out the window.

***

The trip to Eden passed in a haze. Hank didn't remember much of those early days, only what happened when they found sanctuary. Hank stared through the trees. What was he looking at? Was it really a village? His breath caught in his throat. For a brief second, while he glanced at the people near the river, he saw Gladys. She waved at him, beckoning him to come down. Tears clouded his eyes, and he blinked them away. When his vision cleared, she was gone, but they found their salvation.

The place wasn't called Eden at first. It was actually some resort constructed into the side of the mountain. It had a main lodge along with several outlying cabins. There were three people there when they arrived: the cook and two guests. Apparently, the resort was a week away from closing for the season when the attacks started. These were the last people there. They decided to stay for their own safety. They ran out to meet the truck as it pulled into the dirt drive. Worry wrinkled their faces.

"Is it true?" a man asked. He looked about forty with salt-and-pepper hair and round glasses on a smooth-shaved face. "Have zombies really attacked?"

Duke barely had one leg out of the truck. The man held onto his door. Duke slid out and placed a hand on the man's shoulder, taking a deep breath. "It's true. The dead have risen from their graves."

The group collectively gasped. Hank stood on the opposite side of the truck, watching as they gathered around.

"We heard about it on the radio," the man explained, "but we didn't want to believe it."

"That was a week ago," a woman chimed in. She must have been the man's wife because she walked up to him and wrapped her hands around his arm. "We haven't heard anything for days."

Duke nodded, laying his arm on the doorframe. "Yeah, the cities got hit the hardest. I don't really know what's going on out there, but I'm glad to be away from it." He gestured toward Lana and Hank. "Ran into these two about a week ago. Doesn't seem like too many people are left. You haven't had any trouble here?"

They shook their heads in unison.

"Huh." Duke looked at Lana and Hank, smiling.

The people helped the three of them settle in. The man introduced himself as Stan, his wife was Hilary. They learned the other one's name too, but Hank couldn't remember it. Lana high-tailed it to the shower. She couldn't wait any longer. Hank indulged in his own bathing, finishing before Lana, so he waited for her on the little porch. They were going to dinner. She stepped out of the front door wearing a pair of sweats, her hair wet, looking kind of like a drowned rat. She had lost some weight. Her eyes looked sunken in. Her mouth turned down in a frown, and her face was a little pale. He didn't say anything out loud, of course. He might have been a little senile, but he wasn't stupid.

He shook his head. No one deserved this. No one deserved to be hunted by the undead, especially someone as wonderful as Lana. She was so young. But as he watched her, he noticed a spark in her eyes. The same spark he used to see in Gladys's eyes before she went to the home. The spark of hope and love. Lana walked up to him and wrapped her arms around his shoulders, giving him a brief hug.

"You ready?"

"I am."

They headed to the main cabin and joined the others for dinner.

The smell of roasted meat and fresh vegetables was the most enticing thing Hank experienced, especially after eating canned food for days. The way the meat melted on his tongue was divine. For desert, they had cheesecake–his favorite. If he didn't know better, he would have thought he'd died and made it to Heaven. But he knew better. He wasn't in Gladys's arms. He was still alive.

After the dishes were done, Duke stoked a fire in the hearth in the middle of the main cabin, and they all sat around staring into the flames. No one spoke for a long time. Everyone was lost in their own thoughts. Finally, Duke broke the silence.

"I think we should head into other towns, see if there are any more survivors."

Hilary straightened up, color draining from her face. "Do you think that's a good idea? I mean, there are still zombies roaming around."

Duke sighed. "Eventually we're going to have to. We're not going to have food forever."

"As it stands right now," the resort's cook–Hank thought her name was Peggy or something–began, "we have enough food for three weeks." A look of helplessness crossed her face. "It's mainly nonperishables. We were closing for the season. We have maybe a few nights of meat left."

"And then what?" Duke waited a few moments for a response. "We hope the zombie threat has just dissipated? And what if there are others who need help? They might not have three weeks."

Hilary shook her head, rubbing her hands on her thighs. "I don't think it's a good idea. We don't know how bad the threat is."

"Deuteronomy thirty-one verse six says, '*Be strong and courageous. Do not be afraid or terrified because of them, for the Lord your God goes with you; he will never leave you nor forsake you.*' Psalm twenty-seven verses one through three says, '*The Lord is my light and my salvation – whom shall I fear? The Lord is the stronghold of my life – of whom shall I be afraid? When evil men advance against me to devour my flesh, when my enemies and my foes attack me, they will stumble and fall. Though an army besiege me, my heart will not fear; though war break out against me, even then will I be confident.'"* Duke took another deep breath. "I'm not asking any of you to go with me. I know what kind of threat is out there, and I don't want anyone to put themselves in harm's way, but I have to go. I have to ensure our survival and the survival of any of those who are still out there." His gaze drifted from the group to the flames.

Hilary glanced at her husband, gesturing with her head, but Stan averted his gaze downward. Lana stared at Duke. The spark flared in her eyes. She stood from her seat and sat next to him on the couch.

"I'll go with you, Duke."

He smiled and nodded, then pulled out his Bible and read silently to himself.

The room drifted back into silence. Stan messed with something on his shoelace while Hilary picked dirt from under her nails. The cook excused herself to get stuff ready for breakfast. Lana read the Bible over Duke's shoulder. Hank figured Duke would say more, maybe thank Lana for volunteering, maybe formulate a plan. He didn't, and his silence was none of Hank's business. He probably knew what he was doing. Hank found a brochure about the resort on the coffee table in front of him and picked it up.

The whole place was self-sufficient, with its own power generation and water supply. It didn't depend on civilization for anything but food. Even if they ran out of food, there were always options. Open fields in the mountains would be perfect for grazing livestock, and places in the yard could support a garden and chicken coops. Not to mention the wild game that inhabited the mountain. Food wasn't going to be an issue. The whole world could regress into the Dark Ages, and they'd still have running water and electricity. It was amazing.

Hank contemplated the ingenuity of it all before getting awfully tired. It was time to head back to his room. Throwing the pamphlet back where he found it, he attempted to push himself up from the leather chair, but his butt was stuck in the cushions. He couldn't get out. Lana grabbed his arm and helped him to his feet.

"Thanks. I think I'm going to turn in now."

She smiled and held onto his elbow. "Let me walk you to your room."

Hank patted her hand. "I'll be all right. You stay here and enjoy the company."

She shook her head. "I don't mind. I could use some fresh air."

They stepped into the cool night air. Their breath puffed out of their mouths in white clouds. Frost formed on the boardwalk. He looked up at the stars.

"Gonna get real cold here soon."

"Yes, it is." She pulled his arm gently and they stopped. "Do you think Duke is crazy?"

Hank dropped his gaze from the sky to her face. "I think Duke is doing whatever he has to do to make sense of the situation."

"Do you think I'm crazy for wanting to go with him?"

Hank stared at her, his head cocked to the right. He wanted to tell her no, that she volunteered to do what she had to, too, but that wasn't true. She was crazy. She was too young and had too much ahead of her, but she wouldn't listen to an old man. She had already made up her mind. She just needed validation. He stuck his hand in his pocket and wrapped his fingers around Gladys's ring. He sighed.

"I think it doesn't really matter what I think."

His comment hurt her. Her bottom lip pooched out in a pout, her shoulders slumped slightly.

"Of course it matters. If you don't think I should go, I'll stay here."

He chuckled. "And do what?"

"Take care of you."

Hank huffed. "I can take care of myself. Been doin' it for most of my life." He placed a hand on her upper arm. "Though I do appreciate the thought. No, I think Duke needs you more than I do."

Lana's face lit up and she straightened her shoulders. They continued to Hank's cabin. He opened the door and was about to step in when she stopped him again.

"You know," her voice had a dream-like quality to it, "I'm really beginning to believe Duke was right about this whole Eden thing."

"Yeah, I suppose it's worked out well for him."

Confusion crossed her face. "You don't believe God led us here?"

He gestured to the inside of the room. "Why don't you come in? We can talk about this where it's warm."

Lana took a seat on the edge of a brown recliner. Hank threw a few more logs onto the smoldering pile before sinking into the loveseat.

"As I'm sure you well know, God has a plan for everyone. We don't always see it or know what it is, but we trust that He does. It took Duke a while, but he finally found his place in the world. Same goes for you."

She averted her gaze to her lap. "Yeah, but if I had seen it or known it before, I might not be where I am now. If I hadn't turned my back on God, I would be spared having to deal with the living dead."

He shrugged. "Maybe. Maybe not. Maybe you still have work to do."

She looked up. "What about you? What do you think you did to endure this punishment?"

"I don't think I did anything. I don't think I'm being punished."

"Then why didn't you get saved? Do you believe in God? Did you turn your back on Him like I did?"

He sighed and stared at the fire. "No to all of the above. I've always been a religious man, a very devout Christian. I just don't go to church or read the Bible like you and Duke. God and I worked out our own deal of how I would worship Him a long time ago. And to be honest with you, I think I was supposed to die in the fire with my wife. I think I was supposed to be saved, but at the last minute, God had different plans for me."

Lana's eyes widened and she moved further to the edge of her chair. Hank thought she might fall off. "What do you think they are?"

He sighed. "I don't really know, but I trust He knows what He's doing."

She opened her mouth to speak, but then closed it again without saying a word. She focused her gaze on the fire. They sat in silence for a long time.

"I do believe God led us to Eden and salvation," she spoke quietly. "And I think it is only right we find others to share it with."

"That is a very noble gesture."

She stood from her seat and headed to the door. She stopped with her hand on the handle. "Good night, Hank."

"Good night, Lana."

***

Hank woke late the next morning, close to 9:30. He placed his arms out to his sides and stretched. His back popped, his muscles pulled. Pain pinched his face. Sleeping in the truck had stiffened his body more than he realized. It would take a few days to recover, then he'd be fine. Until then, he needed to take some painkillers. After dressing, he headed to the main cabin to find some medicine.

The air was cool as he stepped onto the boardwalk. Frost still lingered in the shade, a fog hung over the mountain. Lana and Duke stood in the courtyard between the cabins, each holding a machete out in front. Hank stopped to watch.

"The most important thing is to make sure you have a good foundation," Duke explained. "If you lose your balance and fall, a zombie has the advantage."

Lana's face paled slightly. She nodded, turning her feet into the ground to plant then firmly.

"Now, raise the machete over your shoulder like this." Duke raised his weapon over his right shoulder. "And swing." He sliced the blade through the air.

Lana mimicked his motion. As the blade came around her back side, she faltered and lost her footing, which also caused her to lose her grip on the machete. It sailed behind her, clanging onto the ground. Lana gasped, bringing her hands up to her mouth.

"It's all right." Duke picked it up. "That's why we're practicing now. You can do that here, just don't do it in battle."

He placed the sword back in her hand, then stood behind her, showing her a better way to grip the weapon. His mouth was right next to her ear, and he spoke softly. Hank couldn't hear what was being said. He frowned. Lana needed to learn how to protect herself, but she shouldn't be getting ready to cut off zombie heads. She should be getting ready to go to dances and passing notes to her friends in class. Hank watched for a few minutes longer as Duke showed her where to place her feet and how to swing the machete. His stomach growled, so he headed toward the main lodge.

After breakfast, Hank decided to go back to his room and take a nap. His body was still incredibly sore, and he needed to catch up on the rest he missed while in the truck. Duke and Lana were no longer in the courtyard. Small pops echoed in the distance. They must have moved to a safer location to practice firing a gun. He shook his head before heading back to his room.

Duke and Lana practiced fighting for a week, close to 8 hours a day. Hank watched every day, sometimes giving advice and showing them both quick ways to load their guns. Lana gained confidence. Her face took on a determined look, and Hank saw her practicing by herself long after the sun went down. He felt confident she'd be able to take care of herself.

The others at the resort helped get together survival packs of food, clothes, and blankets and helped Duke pack his truck. Stan acted like he wanted to go with them, but always came up with some excuse for why he had to stay.

Hank wanted to go, but knew that was impossible. He couldn't move like he used to, or hear, or remember, and it wasn't worth the risk. Duke would probably let him go, but he didn't bring it up, so Hank didn't either. Despite Lana's new-found fighting skills, Hank worried about her. She was so young and inexperienced. Even with Duke's lessons and supervision, anything could happen. Hank hoped she used common sense and stayed out of trouble.

The night before Duke and Lana were supposed to leave, Hank had a hard time sleeping. Nightmares portrayed Gladys and him at home, eating dinner, when someone rings their doorbell. Gladys insists she'll answer it, and he keeps trying to convince her to finish her food. Eventually, she gets up and heads for the door. She rounds the corner, the door hinges squeak as she opens it, then she screams. Hank runs to help her, but it's too late. Macy is there with her worthless boyfriend, and they are gnawing on his wife's insides.

He woke in a cold sweat. Stepping into the bathroom, he turned on the faucet and splashed his face with water. Liquid dripped from his chin as he stared at his reflection. Through the mirror, he saw Gladys sitting in the chair in the other room. She knitted, humming to herself.

"It's not me you're worried about," she spoke in a singsong voice. "You know I'm safe."

"I know." He turned and walked back to bed. The room was empty.

Hank attempted to go back to sleep, but every time he closed his eyes, there was Gladys's face, her lifeless eyes staring at nothing, blood smeared on her cheek. His stomach churned. He threw off the covers and headed to the main cabin for antacids.

A fire blazed in the fireplace, and Duke sat in front of it. Hank found the First Aid kit and downed two Tums before heading back to the main lounge. He sat across from Duke, who had his Bible on his lap and his eyes closed. Hank didn't know if he was sleeping or praying. Either way, he remained silent, not wanting to interrupt. After a few minutes, Duke stirred. He looked at Hank and smiled.

"Hello, Hank. What keeps you up this time of night?"

He patted his chest with a fist. "Heartburn. You?"

"Just looking for guidance."

"You having second thoughts about heading into zombie territory?"

He shook his head without hesitation. "Not at all. James two verses fourteen through seventeen. '*What good is it, my brothers, if a man claims to have faith but has no deeds? Can such faith save him? Suppose a brother or sister is without clothes and daily food. If one of you says to him, 'Go, I wish you well; keep warm and well fed,' but does nothing about his physical needs, what good is it? In the same way, faith by itself, if it is not accompanied by action, is dead.'* I have to go, Hank. I have to help others." His voice softened. "If there's anyone left to help."

"What about Lana? Do you think she feels the same?"

He nodded. "I think Lana is trying to restore her faith, to make up for past wrongs. To her, this is the best way she knows how."

"The only past wrong Lana did was turn her back on God, stop believing in Him. She doesn't have to make up for anything."

"You're probably right, but in her mind, she's failed. She can't restore her faith if she feels like she failed."

"You'll take care of her, right? Make sure she's safe?"

Duke stared at him for a moment. "Of course I will. If I thought she could get hurt or worse, killed, I would never let her go. Despite my faith in God, I'm still human. I need help. Lana was just kind enough to volunteer."

Hank huffed. "Yeah, but you could've made someone else go. You could have told Stan he didn't have a choice. Or what about the cook? What's her name? She looks like she can take care of herself."

"But they wouldn't be any good to me. They would probably freeze up or run away at the first sight of a zombie."

"You don't know Lana won't do that."

"True. But I have faith she'll do the right thing." He took a deep breath. "Hank, I know you're worried about Lana. I know how important she is to you, and if it makes you feel better, I'm scared too. I have read Deuteronomy thirty-one verse six over and over.

'*Be strong and courageous. Do not be afraid or terrified because of them, for the Lord your God goes with you; he will never leave you nor forsake you.*' But, I find I can't shake my fear." He averted his gaze to his lap. "I feel like *I've* failed before I've even started."

Hank clicked his tongue on the roof of his mouth. "You haven't failed anything. It's perfectly natural for you to be afraid. You *should* be afraid. Fear is what will keep your mind alert and your sense of survival humming. I would be worried if you weren't afraid. Do you think Moses wasn't scared to death when the rains started? How do you think Job felt during his tests? If you give your fear to God, He will make sure you stay safe."

Duke looked up at him, his eyes glistening with tears. "Thank you."

He fanned a hand at him. "Don't worry about it. Just make sure both you and Lana come back." He pushed himself out of the chair. "I'm going back to bed. Good night."

Hank climbed back into bed and snuggled under the covers. As he closed his eyes, he felt Gladys's breath on his cheek. He drifted to sleep and saw her face bathed in sunlight. She smiled as she pulled him into her arms and kissed him passionately.

Duke and Lana left before dawn, hoping to make it to a town just as the sun rose and zombies still moved like erosion. A dusting of snow covered the ground, and their breath hung in the air like fog. All of the survivors came to bid them farewell. They finished packing the truck and faced them.

"Well," Duke told them, "we're ready."

"Good luck." Stan clapped Duke on the shoulder. "You know I'd be there with you if I could."

Duke nodded in response.

Hank stepped up to Lana. She gave him a long hug.

"You be careful out there."

"I will."

"I mean it. I need you to come back in one piece." He reached into his pocket and pulled out Gladys's ring. Taking her hand in his, he dropped the diamond in the palm of her hand. She brought her hand to her face to look at it.

"What's this?"

"It's Gladys's wedding ring."

She extended her hand toward him, the ring between her fingers like it would burn her. "I can't take this. It's too important. It means too much to you."

He wrapped his hand around hers and pushed it toward her chest. "Which makes it all the more important that you bring it back to me. Think of it as a good luck charm."

She looked at it again, then placed it on her right ring finger. It fit perfectly. "I'll bring it back. I promise." She hugged Hank again before climbing into the truck.

They all waved as the truck drove down the dirt road. He stared after it for a long time after it was out of sight.

"She's going to be just fine," a voice whispered.

"I know she will. You'll take care of her, won't you, Gladys?"

A breeze stirred, rustling his hair and washing a sense of peace over him. He went back to his room, knowing Duke and Lana were in good hands.

DUKE'S DISCOVERY

Duke didn't want to go back out into zombie-infested cities. What glory was there in putting himself at risk? He would have been content to stay in Eden and wait out the plague. He especially didn't want to take Lana with him, but were there any other choices? Eventually, they were going to run out of food. No one else volunteered to gather supplies. Even if worse came to worse, the people at the resort would probably eat one of their own before leaving the safety of the cabins. But Duke couldn't blame them, and it wasn't his place to judge them. Was there a correct way to react to a zombie uprising?

He and Lana drove to a town about 20 miles east of the resort that had a population somewhere in the couple thousands. With it being only 20 miles away, they were kind of surprised they didn't see any zombies on the road. They thought for sure a wandering one would have happened onto the resort. But since they had no idea how the creatures tracked or what their motivation was, they couldn't explain their lack of encounters. They didn't mind, they were very happy to be left alone. Duke was pretty sure God's grace kept them safe.

It took about 30 minutes winding through mountain roads to get to the outskirts of town. He stopped to scope out the place before entering. He climbed out of the truck to get a better view. The town was set up in a grid system. Downtown had boardwalks and storefronts designed to look like the Old West. Several cars were parked on the streets in front of businesses, houses were closed up, and nothing moved. That worried him. Not even a zombie milled idly around town. They might have left in search of food or whatever it was zombies needed, but Duke figured a few would remain. Using binoculars, he carefully scrutinized every house and window he could see from his vantage point. Everything was dark, still.

"Does it look safe?" Lana whispered next to him.

He wiped his hand over his mouth. "Yeah."

"Then what are we waiting for?"

"I don't know. Something doesn't feel right."

"So, then let's move on. If you don't like this place, it's probably for good reason. There are other towns."

Duke took a deep breath and lowered the binoculars. Lana was right. If it didn't seem safe, they shouldn't chance going into town and possibly getting killed. They were taking a big enough risk being outside Eden. They didn't need to make it worse by going into a dangerous situation. He took another breath.

"Okay. Let's check out the map."

Lana headed toward the truck and was halfway there before he moved to follow her. As he turned, movement caught the corner of his eye. Instinctively, he crouched and stared at the town. At the hardware store, someone or something slowly opened the front door. Duke saw a hand and arm through the glass. It cracked the door before tossing something out. There was a small spark, and then the air filled with pops. Lana ran back to his side.

"What's going on?"

He shook his head.

The sound of moaning deafened the fireworks as zombies from all corners of town converged on the street. There were at least 20 undead. They moved slowly, almost painfully, in the cool morning air. They gathered in a circle, and the door to the hardware store flew open. Two guys armed with machine guns fired into the crowd. Body parts and ichor flew everywhere, staining the concrete and anything within 30 feet. Another person held position on the roof, also armed with a machine gun. The groaning was quickly replaced with maniacal laughter. Lana and Duke watched until the last zombie fell. The two guys on the street gave each other high fives and gave their buddy on the roof a thumbs up.

"Uh," Lana gagged. She paled and swayed back and forth. Thinking she would pass out, Duke grabbed her shoulders.

"Take some deep breaths. It'll be fine."

The guys hooted and hollered. Duke and Lana weren't the only ones who heard them. Another wave of creatures lumbered toward them. It wasn't nearly as many as it had been before, only about 10 or 12, but they were still outnumbered. The guy on the roof noticed them first. He yelled at his friends. They turned, ready to fire their weapons. The first guy got off three shots before running out of ammo. The second didn't shoot any. The guy on the roof fired enough shots so they could get back inside the building. They ducked in and closed the door behind them. The creatures pounded weakly on the door.

"Okay. Now we know there are people down there. We should probably see if they need any help."

Lana's eyes widened. "Well, from that display, I would have to say no, but I could be wrong. What's your plan?"

"Well, I thought we would drive down there and ask if they need any help."

"With zombies down there? Shouldn't we try to draw them away?"

He contemplated for a moment. "We'll probably be safe in the truck, but that's not a bad idea. We can get them to head for us up here, then run over as many as we can. We know they are attracted to sound, so we just have to make enough for them to hear. With any luck, the guy on the roof will see us and signal his friends inside the store."

Lana walked to the truck. "Let's get this over with."

Duke revved the engine for a few minutes, trying to draw the zombies' attention. The guy on the roof heard him, too. His head popped up and he waved. At first, only a few undead moved toward them, but eventually, they all migrated. Duke waited until they were a fair distance from the hardware store, then gripped the wheel and pressed the gas pedal, keeping his foot on the brake. He felt 17 again, when he used to drag race on dirt roads by his house. Lifting his foot off the brake, they lurched forward through squealing tires and burning rubber. He glanced at Lana. Her foot was braced against the dashboard, and her hand gripped the handle above her head. Duke smiled.

The zombies didn't even know what hit them. They took out four, coating the truck in blood and body parts. Others got away unscathed, but followed after them. Their interference gave the guys enough time to get their guns reloaded. They jumped out of the store. Shots echoed in rhythmic fashion as they cut zombies down. Their laughter was barely audible over the rat-tat-tat of guns. Duke slammed on the brakes and the truck skidded to a stop. His heart pounded. His hands dripped sweat. He hadn't had that much fun in weeks. Lana cautiously let go of the handle and put her foot on the floor.

Duke stepped out of the truck just as the last zombie fell. He glanced at the gore surrounding him. Body parts and blood covered the sidewalk and street. A few hands still twitched, legs spasmed. Duke said a quick prayer, then turned his attention from the gore. The guys stared at him with brows furrowed.

"Hi." His hand was extended for them to shake. "I'm Duke."

"Whatcha doin' here, Duke?" one of the boys asked. His strawberry blond hair fell into his eyes, and he probably wasn't older than 19. The other had shoulder-length black hair parted in the middle.

"My friend Lana and I are searching for survivors." He motioned over his shoulder and watched their eyes follow where he indicated.

They both smiled.

"I'm Todd and this is Billy. The one up top is Brad." Blondie pointed to each one. "We didn't really think there were too many others around."

Lana walked around the front of the truck and stood next to Duke. "Did you live in this town?"

Billy nodded. "Yup. Last ones left. Didn't have anywhere else to go, so we decided to stay and do a little cleanup."

Todd laughed, and the two bumped their fists together.

"Why didn't you take one of these cars? Head someplace safe?" Lana folded her arms across her chest.

"And go where?" Billy asked. "From what we understand, everywhere has been overrun with the undead. At least here we know the layout of the town and how to get from one place to another undetected."

"Haven't you thought about finding other survivors?" Duke placed his hands on his hips.

"For what?" asked Todd.

"I don't know. Maybe pool your resources and fight the zombie threat."

"That's exactly what we're doing," Brad called down from the roof. "We just didn't leave town to do it."

"And what are you going to do when all the zombies are dead?" Duke inquired.

Todd and Billy stared at each other for a moment before shrugging.

"I dunno," said Todd. "We really didn't think that far ahead."

Duke shook his head and chuckled. "Well, if you want, we've set up a sanctuary at the resort west of here. I'm sure you know the place."

They nodded.

"You're more than welcome to head back there with us."

"Brad," Billy called, "Come down here. We need to talk."

The three of them disappeared into the store. Duke saw their outlines through the glass. Leaning against the truck, hands in his pockets, he waited. Lana examined the vehicle.

"This is going to be a mess to clean up." She scowled at the ooze on the hood.

Duke pushed himself away from the truck and walked around the front. A hand poked out of the grill, so he kicked it with his foot. It didn't move, so with the nails on his thumb and forefinger, he pulled it out of the metal. He dropped it onto the ground. Dang! There were a lot of dents in the front of the truck.

"Yeah, probably not the best planning. Looks like I did some minor damage to the grill."

Her eyes widened in mock horror. "Oh, my gosh. We wouldn't want to hurt the fluorescent green paint job. It might lower the visual appeal of the truck." She giggled.

Duke smirked. "Ha, ha, ha."

The boys emerged from the store carrying duffel bags and a few more guns. They lined up and faced Duke and Lana.

"We'll go with you to the resort," Billy said, "but we want to help find more survivors."

"With our skills," Brad chimed in. "No zombie stands a chance."

Duke's smirk turned into a smile. "Sounds like a plan. Do you have any idea where we should look first?"

The boys piled into the back seat and directed him to a town several miles south. They rounded the bend. This town hadn't fared as well as the last. Fires blackened half the houses, and zombies freely roamed the streets. A group of them surrounded a two-story hotel downtown.

"I'm guessing there are survivors in there." Duke pointed out the windshield. "I don't know what else would keep the zombies' attention like that." He looked at Lana.

She nodded. "I bet you're right. Plan?"

Billy leaned forward. "We need to draw them away from the building first. Maybe into the field over there." He pointed to an area that had been cleared by flames. "Then, we'll take out as many as we can with our guns."

"There has to be a hundred undead," Lana said. "You can't take them all out."

Billy shook his head. "We don't have to take them all out. We just have to keep them distracted long enough so you two can get whoever's inside the building. Once you get them, come back and pick us up."

Duke sighed. "It's dangerous. There's nothing out there for cover." He didn't want to risk anyone's lives unnecessarily, no matter how good they were with a gun.

Todd huffed. "Dude, we don't need cover. I don't know if you've noticed or not, but we can move faster than zombies."

"Yeah, but if they surround you..."

"They're not going to surround us. We know what we're doing," Billy assured him.

Duke shrugged. What could he do? They had to get the survivors out of the building. He knew they didn't have enough ammo to take every one of the zombies down. What if more emerged from other parts of town? They had to chance it. If things looked dangerous or it wasn't going to work, he'd pick the guys up and they'd formulate a new plan.

"Okay. I'll drive over there. You guys climb out. I'll wait until the zombies are coming after you, then head toward the hotel. You guys have enough ammo?"

They nodded enthusiastically and readied their weapons.

Duke angled the car off the highway. Bumps threw them around the cab. Peoples' belongings littered the ground. It didn't take long for the zombies to discover them. Howling, they limped after the truck. He stopped in the middle of the field and waited. The creatures were about one hundred yards away. The boys jumped out and took strategic positions around the lot. He waited until the undead were within ten yards, then drove to the building, inadvertently running over a few on the way.

Not all of the creatures migrated. Some stayed and feebly attempted to claw their way into the building. Apparently, whatever was inside was more intriguing than the boys. Duke put the truck in park and grabbed his gun. Lana did the same.

"Remember what I told you. Aim and squeeze the trigger. Just relax. Keep your eyes peeled, and we'll get out of this just fine."

The color drained from her face, but she nodded and placed her hand on the handle. Simultaneously, they pushed open the doors and stepped onto the street. They purposely slammed the doors, trying to get the zombies to notice them. It worked, and a few creatures lurched toward them. Duke was ready. He shot the two zombies closest to him. Pow. Pow. They crumpled onto the sidewalk. Lana aimed her gun at a zombie, her tongue sticking out of the side of her mouth. She squeezed the trigger. The bullet hit its mark. The creature collapsed. She looked at Duke and smiled. The color flooded back into her face in a flurry of excitement and adrenalin.

A few more zombies blocked the building's entrance, so Duke took out his machete. Survivors could have been anywhere, and he didn't want to risk a stray bullet hitting someone. Lana stayed outside, watching his back. A zombie approached. He raised his arm. The weapon sliced easily through the creature's neck. The body fell, and Duke turned to his right. The creature's head hit the floor and rolled. Three more were right behind it. The lead creature reached for him. He knelt down and ducked out of the way. Unable to slice the undead's neck, he whacked just below the knee. The zombie fell with a thud. He used the moment to chop off the head before rolling to the left. Another two were on him. He kicked one back, then back somersaulted onto his feet.

The zombie grabbed his arm, his grip cold and clammy. Duke pushed him away to give himself room to swing. There was barely enough time to chop off the head before another lunged for him. The machete clunked into the zombie's skull. The creature's eyes rolled upward and he emitted a squeaky gasp, but he didn't die. With difficulty, Duke pulled the machete out and kicked the zombie in the midsection. He fell. Duke used the opportunity to take off his head.

Dripping with blood and goo, he fought back the urge to vomit. The floor was slippery. His breath was ragged. His arms were sore, and he prayed he'd never have to do something like that again. Lana walked in. Her face lost all color again, and she gagged. She did well, though. Nothing came up, and they went upstairs.

They proceeded with caution. Duke slowly opened the door at the top of the stairs while crouched down. In front of them was a hall littered with blankets and empty cans, as well as a few broken toys.

"Hello? Is anyone here?" Shuffling resounded from a room down the hall. "We're not here to hurt anyone. We just want to help."

Please, God, don't let that be a zombie, Duke prayed.

The third door on the right cracked open before slamming quickly shut. Good sign. Zombies didn't know how to open doors. He signaled to Lana, and they proceeded down the hall to knock softly on the door.

"Hello? My name is Duke. Me and my friend Lana are looking for survivors. If anyone in there is hungry or needs some help, we can supply both."

The door opened slowly. Sun from the window streamed toward them. Duke blinked at the brightness.

When his vision cleared, his breath caught in his throat. Several people huddled in the room. Most of them families with young children, all covered with black ash and wide eyed. He placed the machete in the sheath at his back.

"It's okay. You're going to be just fine."

The rat-tat-tat of machine guns drifted through the window. The boys successfully cut down zombies, but more and more emerged from every corner of town and some from the wilderness. He turned back to the refugees.

"We don't have a lot of time. My friends out there are drawing creatures away from the building, but soon they are going to be surrounded. If you want to go someplace safe, we need to head down to the truck now."

No one argued. They all jumped up, grabbed their sparse belongings and the youngest children, and followed Duke downstairs. Lana took up the rear. When the group made it to the lobby, many of them gasped at the mess. Several children cried. Duke tried to get them through as fast as possible, but he had to make sure the truck wasn't surrounded.

He poked his head out the front door. Quiet. All the undead headed for the decoys. With a sense of urgency, he opened the tailgate and ushered people in. The last of the survivors climbed into the truck when something grabbed Duke's ankle. Surprised, he jerked back, tripping over the curb. He fell backward, bracing himself with his hands. The landing was harder than expected. Pain shot from his wrist into his shoulder. An agonized gasp escaped his mouth. He didn't have time to focus on the injury because hands groped his shins. Wide eyed, he stared at his legs.

A man, wearing a tan corduroy jacket with puffy white lining and a red hat with earflaps, crawled up him. His mouth hung open, ready to bite. His eyes were coated with milkiness. Duke must have run over him because his legs were shredded, bones visible under his tattered jeans.

Duke reached for his gun, but his fingers wouldn't grip the handle. He tried his left hand. His fingers wrapped around the handle when a loud, primal scream stopped him. Lana ran up to him, her eyes flared with intensity, her gaze focused completely on the zombie. Her machete was down at her waist. It arched through the air, and the undead's head tumbled down the sidewalk. The body twitched a little, and the fingers groped at his pants. Duke froze, staring at Lana.

He stared at her for a moment. She panted and kicked the body off him. He should get up and get to the truck, but he couldn't take his eyes off her. She probably weighed one hundred twenty-five pounds and had just decapitated a zombie. Even he didn't get that lucky on his first try. In all fairness, though, the blades had been sharpened before they headed out, which had a lot to do with it. Plus, the zombie was half-rotted, so there wasn't much to cut through. Still, she saved his life. It didn't matter what factors played into it. Without her, he would have been dead. Or bitten. The intensity with which she accomplished it was astounding. Determination, along with something he couldn't place, shrouded her face. She helped him to his feet, and they finished loading survivors.

The back of the truck was full. Survivors sat on each other's laps. Lana closed the tailgate cover, and helped Duke into the passenger seat. The pain in his wrist turned into flames that steadily crawled up his arm. He couldn't drive. Thankfully, Lana climbed into the driver's seat. The truck roared as she stamped on the gas. The sound drew a few undead after them. She drove right through them. She hit one so hard it flew over the hood and slid off the windshield. Her knuckles were white as she gripped the wheel. She sat slightly forward in her seat, her gaze fixed with a deadly intent out the front window.

She hit the field so fast, Duke almost bounced out of his seat. Squeals and thuds came from the back of the truck. Was everyone all right? She drove a few yards past the guys and slammed on the brakes. The three of them ran to the truck and jumped in. They closed the door just as the first wave of zombies slammed into the side. They pounded on the vehicle, rocking it slightly. Lana peeled off, throwing dirt and rocks in her wake, and headed for the highway.

When they were clear of town, she pulled over. She slid the truck into park and looked each one over.

"Is everyone all right?" She pointed at Duke's wrist, which he cradled in his lap. "How's your arm?"

He held it up for her to see. What could he tell her? The pain was excruciating. It was probably broken. However, he didn't want to say it out loud. He didn't want it to be true.

"We need to get some ice on your wrist. It's swelling. Billy, slide open the back window and see how they are back there."

Billy complied. A man poked his face through.

"We're all right. A little shaken up and some minor bruises, but we're alive."

Lana sighed. "Good. There's some water and food in those bags back there. Feel free to help yourselves."

The window slid shut and Lana turned around. She placed both hands on the steering wheel, ready to go, but hesitated. Todd set a hand on her shoulder.

"Lana, are you all right?"

To Duke's surprise, her hands shook and she burst into tears. The four of them sat silently, dumbfounded, staring at her. She pulled herself together a few minutes later, sniffing and wiping her nose on the back of her hand.

She forced a smile. "I'm okay now."

"You sure?" asked Brad. "Do you want one of us to drive?"

She nodded. "Yeah. That might be a good idea." She opened the door and switched seats with her.

Duke glanced over the seat as they headed down the road. Todd had his arm around her shoulders. She leaned against him, tears running down her face. He turned back around quickly. For some reason, anger flared in his chest. He took deep breaths, trying to relax, and closed his eyes. It didn't seem plausible, but he was jealous. There was no reason to be jealous, but the feeling was there. Lana needed comfort, and he wasn't there to give it to her. He could've been, but wasn't. Instead, some kid, some *stranger*, beat him to the punch. Why would that bother him? He owed her for saving his life, for sure, but didn't he save hers? Shouldn't they be even? No, that wasn't it. It was something more.

He felt a connection to her. They spent three days in a truck, and he saw her doubt and frustration turn into hope and enchantment. He helped her regain her faith in God. He spent close to eight hours a day teaching her how to fire a gun and swing a machete, her body right next to his. She turned from a frightened girl into a confident survivalist because of his intervention and actions. A desire to help her through other life obstacles weighed on his shoulders. He could talk to her. He took another deep breath and said a prayer, asking God to give him strength and guidance.

They pulled into Eden, and Brad turned the truck off. Climbing out, he stared in awe at the surroundings. The others stepped out and stood next to him. Lana walked to the back. Duke stood by his door and watched the boys.

"Dude," Billy said, "We have lived twenty miles from this place all our lives, and I have never really seen it. It's awesome!"

Hank, Stan, Hilary, and Peggy came out of the main cabin and helped the survivors unpack. Hank directed them to the lodge and told them to find a seat, explaining they needed to decide what to do next. Lana placed a hand on Duke's arm, expecting to help him into the building.

"You all right?"

"I am." She tucked a piece of hair behind her ear, averting her gaze to the ground, looking sheepish. "I think the emotion of the whole ordeal just hit me. I wasn't scared when we were at the hotel, but when I got into the truck, I thought about how I could have been killed. It all just hit me at once."

He had an overwhelming desire to hug her, but refrained. Would it cross some unspoken boundary between them? Did she even want his comfort? She wanted him to do something, he saw it in her eyes. Instead, they stood awkwardly, staring at each other, for a few minutes.

"I guess we'd better go inside," she finally said.

"Yeah."

As they stepped through the door, survivors surrounded them with hugs and words of thanks. Several were in tears, the liquid making clean trails on their dirty faces. Duke couldn't suppress a smile. After everyone expressed their thanks and admiration, Peggy headed to the kitchen to prepare some food. Hank attempted to sort out rooms and who everyone was. Duke found a seat on the couch. Lana approached with a bag of ice and set it on his wrist.

"One of the survivors is a paramedic. He's agreed to look at your wrist after taking a shower. He was going to do it now, but I told him not to rush." She wrinkled her nose. "You could stand to clean up, too."

Her lack of concern about his wrist made him feel better. It probably wasn't broken, or the paramedic would be at his side. He appreciated her worry and ability to ease his discomfort. He glanced down. The zombies' blood had dried, staining his clothes an unnatural brown and making them crunchy.

"Yeah, I should probably do that." He stood and went to his room.

Before climbing into the shower, he sat on the bed and opened the Bible. He read 1 Corinthians 3:3. *"You are still worldly. For since there is jealousy and quarreling among you, are you not worldly? Are you not acting like mere men?"*

Feeling a little better, he set the book down and stood to go to the bathroom. The Bible slid onto the floor and popped open. Colossians 4:15. *"Let the peace of Christ rule in your hearts, since as members of one body you were called to peace. And be thankful."*

The warm water felt good on the back of his neck. It took a little longer than normal to clean up with his sore wrist. He tried not to think about Lana. His feelings were justified and human, but there were other things to worry about. Besides, he hardly knew her. When would he find time to get to know her? They had souls to save. He needed to focus on that.

The paramedic looked at his wrist. It was sprained. Thank God it wasn't broken! He immobilized it with an Ace bandage, told Duke to rest for a while, and gave him some Ibuprofen. They gathered for dinner afterwards. Duke wanted to say a prayer, to thank God for His grace and bounty, but how would others react? He bowed his head and said one in his mind. Someone nudged his arm.

"Maybe you'd like to share with the rest of us," Lana whispered.

Duke looked up. The others stared at him, their hands folded over their plates. He cleared his throat.

"Dear Lord, thank you for your protection and for showing us to these people. Thank you for the food we are about to eat. Our thoughts and actions are done to glorify you. Amen."

"Amen."

Peggy prepared a wonderful chicken dish with mixed vegetables, baked potatoes, and rolls. For dessert, she made a fruit pie. The survivors ate quickly but not greedily. They made sure the children had their fill before taking seconds. Smiles and laughter filled the room. Amazingly, no one talked about zombies or what they had been through, but focused on what they had and thanked Duke, Lana, and the boys again for saving them. Duke quietly thanked the Lord for showing them the right path.

After dinner, they all gathered around the fire. They needed to formulate a plan. Duke took his place in front. Lana sat across the room with Billy, Todd, and Brad. They laughed. Lana pushed Billy playfully and said something Duke couldn't hear. He watched for a moment before averting his gaze to the floor. She was young and deserved to be with kids her own age. Duke was twenty-five. Lana surely thought he was ancient. He shouldn't feel that way toward her, and really, why did he? Eight years between two people could be a big deal. It was inappropriate.

Besides, she wasn't even his type. He went after the bad girls, the ones who were easily picked up in bars, ones without morals. Well, he did before he found faith and God. Maybe Lana *was* his type. She was the exact opposite of what he used to look for in a woman. But there wasn't time to worry about it. People counted on him. He cleared his throat and asked everyone to settle down.

"I think we need to figure out what our next step should be."

As a group, they figured that since there had been this many survivors so close to Eden, there had to be more out there. There were six able-bodied men and women from the 20 they found who were willing to go out and find others, along with Lana, Billy, Todd, Brad, and Duke. They decided to find more vehicles, and groups of three would head in different directions. Duke hesitated at first. Did they really need to risk the lives of so many people?

"Every day those people are out there with zombies," Todd pointed out, "is a day closer to their deaths. If they are here, they have shelter, food, and warmth. We know the risks, and we're willing to take them."

The others nodded their agreement. He was right. The people needed to be saved, and they were the only ones in a position to do it. God showed Duke they were capable, so he left it in His hands to ensure their safety.

"We only have probably a month before snow falls," the paramedic explained, "then we'll be trapped in these mountains until spring."

"Perhaps," Hank said thoughtfully, "it would be a good idea for those of us left behind to figure out where to plant a garden. Maybe build a greenhouse. There's a field out there," he pointed out the window on the west side, "that would be perfect for grazing."

"That's not a bad idea," Peggy exclaimed. "We can raise our own food. Then we won't have to depend on scavenging supplies from cities. We can be self-sufficient."

Again, everyone agreed, and conversations erupted around the room on the best way to approach a greenhouse and livestock. A few even volunteered to head into the woods to see what kind of wild game they could find. As night wore on, people headed to bed until Hank and Duke were the last ones left. The fire died down to a few short flames.

"I'm glad you brought Lana back safely."

Duke chuckled. "You didn't need to worry about Lana. She knows how to take care of herself."

He looked at Duke and smiled. "So I've been told. Maybe I should say it was a good thing she was there to protect you."

Duke chuckled again. "Yeah. She was my guardian."

"If I may make a suggestion." Hank's attitude turned serious.

"Sure."

"I think it might be best if you stayed behind on this next trip out. Heal up a bit. You won't be any good to anyone if you head out with a sprained wrist."

He stared at the wrap and sighed. "You're probably right. I should probably stay behind."

Hank smiled. "Good." He rubbed his hands together. "Well, that just about does it for me. I'm off to bed."

Duke told him good night, and then turned to the Bible. Just before it fell open, soft footsteps sounded behind him. Lana smiled and sat on the couch across from him.

"I ran into Hank on the way in. He told me you're planning on staying here this trip."

He nodded.

"It's probably for the best, but I'm gonna miss you out there."

Duke's stomach knotted. His jaw fell slightly open. "You're still heading out? Do you think that's a good idea?"

She knitted her brow. "Well, I can't stay here. People need my help out there."

He didn't know what to say. She was right, of course, but he felt responsible for her, like he needed to ensure her safety. If something happened to her and he wasn't there, he would never forgive himself. But what could he say? What right did he have making her stay? And where were those feelings coming from?

"Don't worry about me. Billy and the boys will make sure I'm safe."

He huffed. "I'm sure they will."

She cocked her head to the side and stared at him for a moment. She waited for him to say more, but he didn't.

"Well, I have an early start tomorrow. I'd better get to bed." She stood and headed for the door.

"Lana."

She turned.

"Please be careful out there."

"I will. Just make sure you pray for our safety."

As soon as she left the room, he bowed his head and asked for her safe passage and return.

The group left the next day, before dawn as usual. Lana piled them into the back of the truck. They headed to Billy and the boys' hometown to get some vehicles. From there, they were heading in multiple directions. No one knew exactly how long they would be gone, but they said they wouldn't come back empty handed. There was livestock around, so those would be easy to capture, but it wasn't just about acquiring animals. They needed food and shelter. With just a month before snow, the group needed to hurry to get a stable built. And they didn't have the supplies just lying around. One of the groups was on a mission to find construction materials. They hoped to be back in two days with supplies. Then, it was right to work. Those left behind were going to map out areas around Eden where stuff should go.

Duke felt a tinge of sadness as Lana backed out of the drive in the fluorescent green and silver truck. She waved and honked before disappearing around the bend. He thought about Psalm 37:28, *"For the Lord loves the just and will not forsake his faithful ones,"* and he knew she would be safe.

***

They returned that night around 9:00. Hank and Duke sat in the main cabin by the fire. They heard the truck before they saw it. He glanced out the window and saw headlights around the bend. Smiling, he turned on the solar lamps and stepped onto the porch.

There was an inordinate amount of blood on the truck. It covered the entire hood and most of the passenger side. Lana sat in the passenger seat. The parts of her face that weren't smeared with blood were pale, and she stared straight ahead. Brad drove. When he shut off the engine, both Hank and Duke immediately stepped up to the passenger side door. Duke pulled it open and touched Lana's arm. She turned to look at him but didn't really see him. The tailgate opened and several people climbed out, but aside from noting their presence, Duke focused his concern on Lana.

"Lana, honey," Hank said. "You all right?"

She nodded mechanically as she climbed out. A slight breeze picked up, small flurries of snow drifted to Earth. She stood by the door, completely covered in dried blood. She looked like Duke did after hacking his way through zombies. His stomach fluttered, his heart leapt into his throat. Lana usually got upset after being around zombies, but now she acted way too strange. Dear God, Duke prayed, please tell me she wasn't bitten. He cradled her face in his hands.

"Lana? Lana?" His voice was loud, just below shouting, as he tried to pull her out of her trance. He gave her a little shake. "Lana!"

She blinked a few times and focused on his face. "We...we couldn't save them all."

She trembled beneath Duke's hands. Her knees gave out. His arms wrapped around her shoulders just as she collapsed. Everyone who had been in the truck surrounded them and stared. Lana broke into sobs.

"They pulled them right out of the back of the truck. We couldn't stop them. There were so many." Her voice trailed off into a whisper.

Hank knelt next to Duke and pushed some hair behind her ear. "It's all right. You're safe now."

She took a deep breath and sniffed.

"Are you hurt?"

She shook her head. "No. I'm fine."

Both Hank and Duke sighed with relief.

"Okay, sweetie," Hank said, "let's get you to your room and cleaned up."

Lana stood and followed Hank to her cabin. Duke watched helplessly as they walked away. His stomach unknotted and his heart sank back in his chest, but a

116

feeling of helplessness drifted over him. He turned to Brad, the boys, and the crowd.

"Well, I suppose we should get you some accommodations."

They followed him into the lodge, and he set them up with rooms.

***

It was close to 11:00 when Lana entered the cabin. Duke stared into the flames, contemplating and praying for an answer about why he felt the way he felt. He just read Proverbs 30:18-19, *"There are three things that are too amazing for me, four that I do not understand; the way of an eagle in the sky, the way of a snake on a rock, they way of a ship on the high seas, and the way of a man with a maiden,"* and felt more lost than ever. He didn't hear her when she came in. In fact, she startled him when she sat down on the couch. He jumped.

"Sorry."

"It's okay." He smiled. "I just wasn't expecting anyone this late."

She lowered her head and folded her hands in her lap. "You must think I'm so weak. You must think I have no business going out."

Duke shook his head. "No. Why would I think that?"

She looked at him, her eyes glistened with tears. "The last two times I went out, I broke down crying. I must seem like such a baby."

117

He sighed. "Lana, I don't think you're a baby. In fact, you're braver than a lot of people I know. It's very scary going out into zombie-infested cities. And you handle yourself beautifully while we're there. Heck, you even saved my life. You've saved a lot of lives."

"When I'm there, I'm fine. But when I'm back in the truck and everyone's safe, I lose control. This is going to sound weird, but I'm actually sad I killed those people. I know they are no longer human, but I still feel bad for shooting them. Plus, today, we lost two survivors to the horde."

"It's okay, Lana. Not everyone is supposed to be saved. And I think it's wonderful you cry for the undead. Someone needs to."

"I know not everyone can be saved," she said, "but that doesn't make it any easier."

Duke sighed. "No, it doesn't."

She snuggled closer to him and rested her head on his shoulder. "Read to me. Something happy. Something uplifting."

He smiled and opened the Bible. Flipping to Psalms, he started reading. As the light of the fire died, the heat from her body radiated through his, and he wanted the moment to last forever.

GOD'S PROMISE

The paramedic's prediction was almost right. It took about six weeks before snow trapped the survivors in Eden. They finished a little bit of the work on the long list of to-dos: they constructed a crude greenhouse, and a couple of cows and some chickens roamed the grounds. No one expected to actually have food the first winter, so they stocked up on canned goods and anything else they could fit into the freezer. Really, it wasn't much because everything outside of Eden spoiled, but canned goods were plentiful. There were one hundred twenty-three survivors, with forty kids who ranged in age from seven weeks to fourteen. The cabins were crowded, but they made do. They had to. Where else could they go? They started some new houses, but they wouldn't be finished any time soon. The weather wouldn't allow it.

***

Lana sat on the floor of the main lodge and planted vegetables. Since it was so cold and they were so small, she started them in inside. She never had a garden before, so she wasn't exactly sure what she was doing. The plants seemed so fragile, so delicate. She was afraid she would snap their stalks putting them into the soil. Hank helped her when he could, which wasn't often since he was busy directing construction. However, he said he trusted her to do it right. She wasn't so sure, but

119

she had to do something since Hank and Duke discouraged her from going out after the last trip. They both thought it best that she stayed in Eden. She fought against it at first, telling them she was okay, that she could handle herself, but they weren't convinced. They thought it was too hard on her psyche. Lana probably could have fought harder or just left, but she didn't. She knew Hank and Duke were just looking out for her, and she respected and owed them too much to be disobedient. Besides, it wasn't in her nature.

Tough didn't describe her last trip out. Brutal and hellish came close. She and the boys left early, before dawn, like always, and headed south into the U.S. As they crossed the border, a strange fluttering entered her stomach. At first, she thought it was nerves, but looking back, it was a warning.

***

Gray clouds covered the morning sky. Snow threatened to fall at any moment. The group stuck to back roads and two-lane highways because they knew they were clear. They happened on a little place with a population of three hundred sixty-four people. Empty. No people and no zombies. They continued south and came to a town that once had a population of over ten thousand. Brad stopped the truck on the outskirts of town and they all stared at vacant buildings. The tingling in her stomach worsened. Although they couldn't see anything moving, they heard zombies moaning.

"I don't think this is such a good idea," Lana told the boys. "We've never swept a place this big before."

Brad rolled his eyes. "It'll be fine."

"How is it going to be fine?" She pointed out the windshield. "The population was over ten thousand. Do you know how many zombies that makes?"

Billy leaned forward and dropped his arm over the back of the seat. "Our machine guns will take care of them. You don't have to worry."

"Yeah," Todd smiled, "we know what we're doing."

She narrowed her eyes to slits. "You know what you're doing when there are less zombies and you're in an area you know. This is new territory."

Brad put the truck in gear. "Either way, we're here. We should at least find out if there's something salvageable. Or anyone who needs saving."

The truck moved forward. Every fiber of Lana's being screamed for her to get out. She placed her hand on the handle, ready to pull, but where could she go? She couldn't just wait for them on the side of the road. Maybe she could find a tree. She glanced out the window. Rolling hills surrounded them, tall mountain peaks framed the horizon, and fields of sagebrush, the tallest of which were maybe five feet, offered little protection. She took deep breaths and tried to stay calm. Loosening her grip on the handle, she laid her gun on her lap, refusing to take her hand off it, her body poised to shoot. It would be all right. Duke trained her for situations like these, and God would ensure her safety. If she remained calm, she would come out alive.

Abandoned vehicles clogged the main street, so Brad drove on sidewalks and through lawns when he could. Progress was slow, and the creatures took an interest in the truck. Lana glanced into the rearview mirror and noticed a group following them. She tried to swallow the lump in her throat.

They drove downtown. In front of the tallest building, which was on old theater, stood a group of zombies. She couldn't even count how many were there. Brad stopped the truck.

"Whoa," he breathed. He glanced over his shoulder and stared at the others. "This should be interesting."

Lana didn't have to look. She knew both Billy and Todd smiled, stroking their weapons, nodding.

"There's a parking lot." Billy pointed to his left. "There are a couple of two-story buildings around it. I'll take position on the roof and Todd can lure them over."

She turned in her seat. "And what's he going to do when the horde gets there? He's a sitting duck on the ground."

Billy lowered his head and thought for a moment. "Okay, change of plan. Both Todd and I will take positions on the roof. You and Brad will lure them with the truck. Once the majority of the creatures are over there, you drive back to the building while Todd and I shoot them."

"Yeah," Todd said, his hand in the air for a high five. "They'll never know what hit 'em!"

She opened her mouth to protest, but before she could say anything, Brad drove to the lot. A few creatures still followed them, attracting more attention from the horde. Billy and Todd barely had time to get out of the truck before the first few zombies converged on their position. Lana couldn't tell if they made it to the roof because yellowed flesh fell off a face pressed to her window, white cheekbone clicked on the glass, the mouth snapped open and closed.

The truck rocked slightly as more creatures found them, each trying to claw their way through the metal. A few shots rang out, and Brad took that as a sign the other two were in position. He floored the gas pedal and pushed through the crowd. The truck bumped and jerked as bodies fell under the tires. Creatures kept coming, their hands scraping against the doors. As soon as they were clear, Lana heard the steady tapping of machine gun fire.

They made it back to the theater. The horde thinned, but it was still overwhelmingly large. How were they going to hack or shoot through them? If they tried, one of them would die. She turned to Brad.

"This isn't going to work. There are too many. We have to go back and get Billy and Todd."

"We might be all right. We have to try. Maybe you should get on the roof and start firing into the crowd."

She stared at him, mouth open. "I am NOT getting on the roof. You must be out of your mind."

He grimaced. "Fine. I'll do it." He grabbed his gun and started to open the door.

Something thudded against the back of the truck. Brad closed the door and glanced through the rearview. Another thud sounded, this one closer to the passenger door. Lana's heart raced in her chest. She propped herself on her knees, her finger on the trigger of her gun, staring out each window. Another thud; this one on Brad's door. He looked out the window. Without saying a word, he put the truck in gear and drove around the block. She wanted to ask what it was, but the color drained from his face and his eyes widened. She didn't want to know.

As they rounded the corner, she saw someone in the window on the second floor of the theater waving a white flag.

"There's someone in there," she told Brad.

"I see them. I just don't know how we're going to get to them."

"It looks like he's signaling something." Lana squinted. "I don't know, pointing to the back maybe?"

"Maybe. Let's check it out."

He turned the corner, and they noticed an alley. A fire escape ran from the top of the building all the way to the ground. The guy from the window popped out on top of the stairs. He waved his flag again. Brad honked.

Lana cringed. It would have been the ideal situation, except a dumpster and several cars blocked the other end of the alley. There was only one way in and out. More than likely, a few zombies already knew they were there, but Brad just alerted a few more.

"Here goes nothin'." Brad pulled up next to the building. "I'll keep watch from the top, you get to the back and open the tailgate."

Without thinking, she opened her door. If she had a chance to think, she would have realized it was a bad idea and made Brad drive out of town. A zombie approached from Lana's right, her mouth twisted open and groaning. Lana raised her gun and squeezed the trigger. The creature dropped. The sound of clanging metal caught her attention. Survivors clambered down the fire escape. She didn't know how many there were, and she didn't stop to count. She hurried to the back.

While opening the tailgate, something touched her shoulder. She turned, expecting to see a survivor, and came face to face with a rotted corpse. Flesh had completely rotted from the thing's face, and one eye dangled from the socket. Lana screamed and jerked back. She attempted to raise her gun, but the creature flailed after her, knocking her arm. She reached around her back, grabbing for her machete. Her fingers touched the handle. The zombie was close–too close. If it could breathe, she would've felt its breath on her face. It grabbed her shoulder. The fingers were bony and sharp.

They dug into her flesh. She inhaled a sharp breath, tugging at the machete. It wouldn't move. She wasn't going to get the blade out in time. Tears threatened to fall. She was going to die.

Footsteps sounded behind her, approaching quickly. The man with the flag whacked the zombie with a bat. The crack of bone on wood was sharp. Lana flinched as he continued to beat the skull until there was nothing left. He turned to her, panting.

"You all right?"

What just happened? Did she really have contact with a zombie? She said a quick prayer and thanked God for saving her life. She turned to the man and nodded. She wanted to thank him for his actions, but the words stuck in her throat. Plus, she had a hard time believing the attack actually happened. Instead, she signaled for them to get in the truck.

People piled in. Brad's machine gun fired. She risked a glance around the front of the truck. A pile of bodies built up in the alley, with new zombies crawling over the fallen ones to get to them. Turning back around, she noticed hundreds of creatures clogged their only way out. Her breath caught. She raised the gun and fired until it clicked. She reached for another magazine but didn't have time to load it.

"We're in. Let's go!"

Lana closed the tailgate and camper shell before hurrying back to the cab. Brad already sat in his seat.

He put the truck in reverse before she closed her door. The thumping and scraping was almost deafening, and, again, the truck bounced as bodies were crushed under the tires. They made it to the street, and Brad put the truck in drive. The tires spun and the smell of burning rubber drifted into her nose. They headed back to the lot.

Bodies littered the ground and blood sparkled in the dreary morning air. Every creature that followed them into the lot had been cut down. As Lana stared at the carnage, snow drifted down and turned pink as it settled on corpses. Her stomach lurched, and she fought to swallow chunks back down. Brad honked the horn. The tailgate opened. She climbed into the back seat and slid open the window. Her hands were sweaty, her heart beat rapidly. Adrenalin coursed through her veins. She fought the urge to run. It was bad enough she and the guys risked their lives. She didn't want the survivors to put theirs on the line.

"What are you doing?"

"Giving them some cover."

She looked out the back window. The undead headed straight for them. There had to be thousands of them, each with their mouths open, hoping for a bite. She placed a magazine into her gun and opened the door. She couldn't hold them off herself, so maybe a little help wasn't so bad. She fired a few shots. God, she prayed, please make Billy and Todd hurry up! It was only minutes, but it seemed like an eternity before they emerged from the building. Zombies were within fifty feet, steadily moving forward. They couldn't linger much longer. She made sure they were in the truck before climbing in after them. She poked her head through the back window.

"They're in. Let's go."

The survivors scrambled back into the bed. Brad put the truck in gear and headed toward safety. They hit a bump, and the tailgate dropped open. Lana watched several of the survivors attempt to pull it closed, almost being bounced out in the process.

"Brad, stop!" she called.

He slammed on the brakes. A creature emerged from a ditch on the right. No one noticed her. They were too concerned with the truck. The man jumped out to push the gate closed, and the zombie latched onto his arm. His scream echoed through the cold air. Another grabbed him from under the vehicle. He toppled backward out of sight. His friend reached for him, trying to pull him back into the truck. The zombie that bit the first man's arm let go and focused her attention on the second.

Lana closed her eyes. She didn't want to see what happened next. The survivors yelled, telling them to go. She heard nails scraping on metal and knew the undead were trying to get in. If she could've forced her eyes open, she would've shot the zombies, but her body refused to cooperate. Brad floored the gas, and they drove out of town.

They stopped on the side of the road and Lana climbed out, unable to hold the bile down. She straightened up, wiping her mouth with the back of her hand. Todd stood next to her.

"There was nothing you could have done. You couldn't save them."

She turned without saying a word and climbed into the front seat of the truck.

***

Lana still saw the man's face sometimes when she closed her eyes, his eyes round and wide, his hands grasping desperately for someone to save him. But she stopped being angry at the boys for his death. She used to tell herself he might still be alive if they hadn't gone there. But she knew that probably wasn't true. Besides, what would have happened to the others? Duke was right. Not everyone could be saved, but Lana wondered what the man had done to survive for so long in the theater only to fall prey to the horde while trying to save his friends. How did he upset God? Did he and his friend do something together? It wasn't her place to question or judge. God had His reasons. It took a few days to reach that conclusion, and Lana thought Hank and Duke took her silent musings for the inability to cope with the stress. That was when they forbade her to venture out. Rather they didn't really forbid her, they just strongly suggested it wasn't a good idea.

In all honesty, she liked to go out. She liked to be reminded how lucky they were and see what could have been. Yeah, it upset her and she cried whenever she came back, but you would have, too. The world was destroyed, obliterated, and corpses roamed free. Was there a right way to react? Maybe just shrug, like it's a daily occurrence? Every time they went out, they risked becoming them. It was scary and exhilarating and nerve wracking all at the same time. Lana had no other way to react to the situation than by crying.

She supposed she could have reacted like Billy or Todd or Brad and just totally lost her mind. They felt nothing. They thought it was a game. They slaughtered people they had known their entire lives and congratulated each other on great shots. Yeah, they were killing zombies, but they didn't hesitate before pulling the trigger. Lana knew it was kill or be killed, but even later, when everything was silent, they still felt nothing.

She didn't know. Maybe she was too sentimental, but it pained her to shoot them. Granted, like the boys, she never hesitated, but she always thought later that she had killed someone. Well, not really a person, but a creature in human form. They had been human at one time. What if they found a cure? Then, all those people she shot would never have a chance to be human again, and it was her fault. Guilt consumed her. She looked for Duke and asked if her feelings were normal.

"First of all, Lana, this isn't some disease or virus that can be cured. Those zombies you shot were zombies, and they won't ever be human again. God understands we must do things to protect ourselves and those we love."

They sat in front of the fire. Everyone else had gone to bed. They were alone. Ever since her last trip out and the night following, when she sought comfort from Duke and the Bible, they spent a lot of time together. It wasn't always necessarily to talk about God, although that happened a lot. Often times, they were together during the day as they did their chores. She told herself she would let Duke teach her all he knew about God, and she enjoyed his wisdom and ability to make her feel better. However, she also found herself wanting to learn more about him.

"Even though murder is against the Commandments, I think He allows exceptions in certain cases." Duke folded his hands over the Bible in his lap. "Besides, as long as you confess your sins, He will forgive you for them."

"I try, but it doesn't always make me feel better."

He smiled. "'*Trust in the Lord with all your heart and lean not on your own understanding.*' Proverbs three verse five. Or, Philippians chapter four verses six through seven. '*Do not be anxious about anything, but in everything, by prayer and petition, with thanksgiving, present your requests to God. And the peace of God, which transcends all understanding, will guard your hearts and your minds in Christ Jesus.'"*

She faced him, pulling her legs underneath her. "I envy you. You make it all sound so simple. I wish I had as much faith as you do."

He chuckled. "Don't envy me, it's a sin. Besides, I have my moments of weakness just like everyone. I just trust the Lord knows what He's doing and I pray. *A lot.*"

"Weakness? What could possibly make you weak?"

"Fear, jealousy, love. You know, the usual stuff."

"Fear I can understand. There's a lot of stuff to be afraid of. And love, yeah, that can be confusing. But I don't understand jealousy. What do you have to be jealous of?"

He shrugged his shoulder. "I am still human, you know. Sometimes I get upset thinking the person I love might love someone else."

Lana stared at him for a moment, trying to figure out if he referred to an actual person or spoke metaphorically. There weren't a lot of women his age around, although there were a few. She tried to remember if she saw him with any of them lately. Could he perhaps be talking about someone older? She ran through the possibilities in her head. As her mind raced, his face turned bright red. His gaze fell to his lap. He cleared his throat.

"Well, anyway. Maybe we should talk about something else."

Lana touched his arm. "No, I'm sorry. I didn't mean to embarrass you. I was trying to figure out who you were talking about."

"I'm talking about you."

She jerked her hand back in surprise. "Me?"

He waved his hand through the air. "Never mind. Don't worry about it. Forget I said anything."

"No. I want to talk about this." She scooted closer to him on the couch. "What have I ever done to make you jealous?"

"Sometimes," he sighed and sat silent for a moment. "Sometimes I think you like Brad or Todd or Billy better than me. After all, they are your age. I know I shouldn't feel this way, and I try to let it go, but sometimes I just can't." He shook his head. "I sound like I'm in junior high."

She laughed. "You're joking right?"

He looked at her, his mouth turned downward. She didn't mean to make him uncomfortable. It was the last thing she wanted, but he surprised her, and she didn't really know how to react. She liked him, a lot, but didn't know how to tell him. He was eight years older. She figured it was weird to be attracted to him. She didn't know, but it was possible he thought of her as a kid. It was a relief to know he felt the same way.

"They aren't even my type." She placed a hand on his shoulder. "And, yeah, you do sound like a seventh grader, but you have nothing to be jealous of." She moved so she sat right next to him and rested her head on his shoulder. "Let's read about Adam and Eve."

Duke opened the Bible and started reading when someone entered the lodge. They both looked up. Todd stood before them.

Lana glanced at Duke. They chuckled.

"Whatcha doing?" Todd asked.

"Reading the Bible," she told him.

"Do you mind if I join you? I can't sleep."

"Not at all," Duke said.

Todd took a seat on the couch opposite of them, and Duke continued reading.

***

Duke never had any intention of becoming Eden's spiritual leader, but did. It started with Todd. Then, a few others came. Eventually, the majority of Eden stayed up late and listened to stories from the Bible. They would have long discussions afterward, sharing personal experiences or opinions about the readings. Lana felt jealous. They encroached on what she believed was her special time with Duke, but, learning from Duke, she tried to push it away and asked God for guidance. He must have heard her prayer because someone suggested Duke change his readings to first thing in the morning so the kids could listen, and so he did. They once again had their evenings free to spend with each other.

Winter eventually turned to spring, and it was about time! Lana was sick of canned meat and craved a berry pie. When the roads cleared, groups organized and headed out to find survivors and supplies. Despite her protests, Duke ventured out into the world. Maybe she didn't protest enough, but she felt like she didn't have any say in what Duke did. She mentioned a few times that she didn't think it was a good idea, but he still had work to do. Who was Lana to stop him? She couldn't be selfish. She knew others needed him just as badly as she did, but she didn't want to share. She did a lot of praying for that too.

When Lana returned from her last trip, Hank gave her his wife's ring. She protested, but he said he didn't have any need of it. His wife remained in his heart and not in the ring. Flattered by his gesture, she promised to take good care of it. When she found out Duke was leaving, she insisted he take the ring.

"It's always brought me luck," she told Duke. "And it will ensure you come back."

He smiled as he placed it on the chain with the cross around his neck. Every time he came back, he tried to return it, but Lana told him she would only take it when he stopped traveling.

***

She sat in the greenhouse, transplanting her new batch of tomato plants, when Duke came through the door. Lana jumped to her feet and threw her arms around his neck. He hugged her back, and they held each other for a long time. When she let go, one of those I-know-something-you-don't-know smiles covered his face. She furrowed her brow.

"What's up with you?"

"Nothing. I just wanted to give you this ring back."

Lana stepped back and held up her hands. "Oh, no. You know the deal."

He immediately dropped to one knee. Her breath caught in her throat.

"If you promise to spend the rest of your days with me as my wife, I promise I won't go out on any more adventures."

Her eyes welled with tears. She gave him the only answer she could.

***

Their wedding occurred on the first day of summer. It wasn't the first wedding, and it wouldn't be the last. By then, the population had swelled to over 200 souls. Houses were being erected up the mountainside, and the pasture was full of sheep and cows. Chickens roamed the grounds by the buildings from the original resort, and a playground had been set up for the kids. The lodge became the main meeting place and school. They were a thriving town.

A group of women made her dress, a simple white gown with scoop neckline, high waist, and poet sleeves. Everyone turned out for the occasion. Hank walked her down the aisle and gave Duke his wedding band so they would have a matching set. As they stepped down the aisle, Hank gently squeezed her hand.

"You look beautiful, Lana. You remind me of Gladys on our wedding day."

"I wouldn't be here if it weren't for you. Thank you."

They stopped at the altar. Lana hugged Hank. He squeezed back and, with tears in his eyes, gave her hand to Duke.

***

Even though Duke stopped venturing out, others still looked for survivors. Every time a group came back, Lana anxiously awaited news from the outside. She knew that any day, they would come back and tell them the zombies had disappeared just as mysteriously as they appeared. She knew it in her heart and from the word of God.

God is not unjust; he will not forget your work and the love you have shown him as you have helped his people and continue to help them. Hebrews 6:10.

You will surely forget your trouble, recalling it only as waters gone by. Life will be brighter than noonday, and darkness will become like morning. You will be secure, because there is hope; you will look about you and take your rest in safety. You will lie down, with no one to make you afraid, and many will court your favor. But the eyes of the wicked will fail, and escape will elude them; their hope will become a dying gasp. Job 11: 16-20.

She knew even when that day came, they would continue to thrive in Eden. After all, it was the Promised Land for God's saved people. They decided as a group their best chance would be to stay in the mountains. Even if the cities were free from undead, there were other dangers they were likely to encounter. God provided them with a new life and a safe haven. He saved them. Who were they to question His will? And why would they?

Meet The Author

Biography

Pembroke Sinclair has had several stories published in various places. She writes an eclectic mix of stories ranging from western to science fiction to fantasy. Her stories have been published in various places, including Static Movement, chuckhawks.com, The Cynic Online Magazine, Sonar 4 Publications, Golden Visions Magazine, and Residential Aliens.

Her novels, ***Coming from Nowhere*** and ***Life After the Undead,*** as well as short stories, ***Weeping Bride (Brides and Dark Secrets Anthology)*** are available at eTreasures Publishing and Amazon.com. Her story, Sohei, was named one of the Best Stories of 2008 by The Cynic Online Magazine.

If you would like to contact Pembroke, she can be reached at pembrokesinclair@hotmail.com or pembrokesinclair.blogspot.com

We hope you have enjoyed this title and we encourage you to check out Ms. Sinclair's other titles available at eTreasures Publishing:

Coming From Nowhere

JD does not have a past--at least not one that she can remember--and that makes living life on Mars challenging.

With nowhere to go, she is sent to the local military academy where she is trained to become a member of the elite secret police. While there, she becomes a pawn in Roger's struggle for military dominance and Chris's rebellion to overthrow the military regime.

She supposedly holds a secret that will change the face of the soldier, but, unfortunately, she doesn't know what that secret is. Her only desire is to find the truth of her existence, and finds herself thrust into a realm where the truth of her past and present is more horrific than she ever imagined.

Life After The Undead

The world has come to an end. It doesn't go out with a bang, or even a whimper. It goes out in an orgy of blood and the dead rising from their graves to feast on living flesh. As democracy crumples and the world melts into anarchy, five families in the U.S. rise to protect the survivors. The undead hate a humid environment, so they are migrating westward to escape its deteriorating effects. The survivors are constructing a wall in North Platte to keep the zombie threat to the west, while tyranny rules among the humans to the east. Capable but naïve Krista is 15 when the first attacks occur. She loses her family and barely escapes with her life. She makes her way to the wall to begin a new life. But, as the undead threat grows and dictators brainwash those she cares about, Krista must fight not only to survive but also to defend everything she holds dear--her country, her freedom, and ultimately those she loves.

Pembroke Sinclair

Death to the Undead

The battle that began in *Life After the Undead* continues.

Zombies changed her life completely...

Tough teenager Krista escaped to the safety of Florida after her parents were killed by the zombie horde. She united with General Liet, a distant cousin, and moved with him to North Platte to help build a wall to keep the zombies in the West. Krista fell in love with Quinn, a survivor and fighter from the zombie-infested wildlands of the West, and together they freed the garrison at North Platte from the power-hungry Liet.

But zombies aren't the only enemy they have to face...

Now, North Platte is free, but Liet was not the only one using the zombie apocalypse to control their people. Florida is ruled by five ruthless Families, who use intimidation and the threat of the zombie horde to coerce their populace. Krista and Quinn hatch a desperate plan to run guns into the state and help the people revolt. Krista and Quinn, labeled as rebels, run for their lives when the Families attack North Platte. The Families want them captured, the zombies want to eat them, and other survivors want them dead. Caught in between powerful forces, they must survive long enough to devise a new plan and put it into action, all while trying to solidify their new relationship and trying not to self-destruct in the meantime.

142

The Weeping Bride

Part of Brides & Dark Secrets Anthology
Paranormal Romance Novella

Scorned at her own wedding, The Weeping Bride has vowed to make every bride from her hometown miserable until she finds her own happiness. When the groom at a friend's wedding disappears, Melanie and Tyler must solve the mystery of the Bride to save him. Time is not on their side. Will they find him before The Weeping Bride's revenge is satiated?

The Way She Makes Me Feel

Drake Steng had it all: a professional football career, money, and looks. Finding women wasn't a problem, having a relationship was. He thought he found true love when he was 12, but as a boy, how was he to know? He never had the courage to find out, and she slipped from his grasp. When Evie walks back into his life years later, he gets a second chance to discover true love, but are Evie and Drake fated to be together or will he lose his courage and lose her again?

###